The Gamble on Love

By Regina Rodgers

Fiction and Literature: Historical Romance

ISBN-13: 978-1-956654-88-2

Chapter One

St. Louis, Missouri
Early May 1875

"Get back here you cheating, yellow-bellied dog!" Dallas Rand darted from the saloon into the street. He took a wide-legged stance, aimed, and fired through a cloud of dust.

Black Jack Brannigan hunkered low over his stallion's neck as a bullet zinged past his ear. A slug creased his flesh. Searing pain shot through his left arm. Jack's heart pounded faster than Ace's hoofbeats as he glanced over his shoulder. Dallas whipped a second six-shooter from his holster and fired again.

Jack gasped, his breath short, ragged puffs as he lashed his stallion's back with the reins. Another bullet whizzed past. He dug his heels into Ace's sides and disappeared around a corner, racing out of town at a break-neck pace.

Gradually, he slowed his lathered horse to a lope, taking an occasional glance over his shoulder. With the

Shady Lady Saloon well behind, Jack reined into a copse of trees. Heaving, he wiped his sweaty brow with his shirtsleeve, ripped it open, and examined his bloody arm. Just a flesh wound, but it burned like the dickens. From his saddlebag, he pulled out a bandana and a bottle of whiskey. He poured it over the wound and then wrapped the cloth around his arm.

Through narrowed eyes, he scanned the skyline. No sign of pursuit. He pressed the bottle to his lips again and threw back a hard gulp, cringing at the fire in his throat.

Once he'd buckled the saddlebags tossed in haste over Ace's back, he patted them with satisfaction. They held at least five thousand dollars. The poker game had paid off nicely. Now, he had his entry fee and, this time next month, he'd ante up at the Grand Championship Poker Tournament in San Francisco. With the hundred thousand dollars he planned to win, he'd build California's finest saloon and gambling establishment.

The thought brought a smile to his face. He took one last swallow of whiskey and nudged Ace onto the road, headed west for California.

~

Independence, Missouri
Two weeks later

Evangeline Gentry stuffed her hands into her pants pockets and watched as Doc O'Brien hobbled on arthritic legs to his supply cupboard. She caught a glimpse of herself when Doc opened the glass door of the medicine cabinet. Hastily, she retwisted her messy bun, tucked her baggy shirt into the top of her trousers, and brushed the dust from her clothes. She shook her head at the reflection and sighed. *I wish I hadn't had to come to town like this. I look like something the dog dragged in.*

Doc caught sight of her embarrassment. "Pretty lady, I brought you into this world twenty-seven years ago. And you're as lovely now as you were then, and twice as sweet."

Evangeline felt her cheeks burn. "Thank you, Doc, but I must look a sight. I was cleaning the chicken coop when Rusty fell, and I probably smell as bad as I look."

Doc smiled and squeezed her shoulder. "Never," he whispered near her ear. He limped past her to stand next to the grimacing ranch hand. "Well, Rusty, it's not broken, but it'll sure be sore for a while." He laid bandages and a sling on the examining table.

Evangeline picked up a damp cloth and dabbed sweat from her ranch foreman's brow. "You're one lucky man, Rusty Cunningham. I thought you'd broken your arm for sure." She patted his shoulder.

Rusty grimaced and pulled away. "Easy there, ma'am. It might not be busted, but it sure hurts like blazes."

Doc O'Brien stood behind Rusty and laid his hands on the young man's shoulders. "It's not broken, but it is dislocated, and I've got to put it back into place. Now, lay down on the floor."

The color drained from Rusty's face, and he growled like a cornered bobcat. "You're gonna do *what*?" Rusty eyed Doc with suspicion but obeyed.

Doc lowered himself to a seated position on the floor and placed a foot in the younger man's armpit.

Rusty moaned as the old man clasped a hand around his wrist.

"You'll be fine." Evangeline brushed his sweaty auburn hair back from his face and wiped his brow again. She cringed as the older man settled into position.

Doc reached up with his free hand, pushed a small metal bowl off the table, and sent it clanging to the floor. At that moment, he shoved slowly against Rusty's armpit with his foot and rotated his arm downward.

She covered her mouth and squeezed her eyes shut. A sickening *pop* filled the room. She flinched and turned away.

Rusty hollered so loud it rattled the windowpane, but his shoulder had moved back into place.

Doc wiped the sweat from his forehead and clambered to his feet. "Mercy, I hate doin' that." He put his hand to his bent back and straightened it.

Rusty's face had turned white as Doc's bandages. "Well, I wasn't too crazy about it myself." He groaned and inhaled deeply, then shrugged his shoulder. He blinked. "But it does feel better."

She snatched a towel from the table and fanned his clammy face. "You doing okay, Rusty?"

Doc raised a bushy, gray eyebrow. "I reckon we both survived it. Now get on the table and let me wrap that shoulder."

Working together, they eased the patient onto the examining table.

Doc's voice was stern. "You're gonna be sore for a while, Rusty. Keep your arm in a sling for a couple of weeks, and I mean all the time. You're on limited duty at the ranch 'til I say otherwise."

"I can't do that, Doc. You know Miss Eva ain't got nobody but me to run things and keep them hired hands in line."

"Don't worry, Rusty," she said. "You have to heal up, don't you? We'll make do." Watching Doc reset Rusty's shoulder sent a wave of queasiness through her. "I think I'll get a breath of fresh air." She rushed out the door.

As she hurried toward the bench in front of the mercantile, glass shattered nearby. She jumped. Heart thumping, she spun toward the noise. Across the street, two men grappled in broken shards on the boardwalk in front of the Golden Eagle Saloon.

A crowd soon gathered to watch the brawl between Caleb Hutchison, a wiry young cowboy, and a taller, dark-haired man. Onlookers shouted and laughed as the two punched and fought their way into the middle of the road.

"Give him a right hook, Caleb!" an old man shouted.

A young woman in the crowd squealed in horror, yet stepped closer.

Caleb grabbed the other man's vest and drew back a fist.

The stranger blocked Caleb's blow and landed a jaw-busting punch to his face.

Mouth agape, she watched as the sinewy cowboy sprang to his feet and lunged. The men wrestled farther into the street which brought their scuffle toward her.

The dark-haired man slammed a sharp uppercut to the young cowboy's chin and sent him sprawling into the dust. He rebounded and charged, grabbing his opponent's shirt collar and drew back again.

Before he could land his blow, Sheriff Dalton tramped onto the boardwalk, and a shotgun blast split the air. Everyone froze.

Young Caleb took advantage of the moment and sucker-punched his opponent, causing the tall man to fall in a heap at Evangeline's feet.

She flinched and let out a gasp.

The crowd hushed, quiet enough she heard a bird chirping in a nearby tree.

The dark-haired brawler stood and unfolded to a height and breadth of shoulders that might have daunted a more timid woman. The stranger brushed the dust from his pants and straightened his richly threaded brocade vest. "Ma'am." He swayed as he stepped forward and offered his hand. "The name's Jack Brannigan."

After a brief hesitation, she extended her hand.

He took it, bent as if to kiss it, but he stopped short, his eyes fastening onto her dirty work boots. He straightened and took his sweet time as his bold gaze traveled up her body, past the baggy trousers and old work shirt, until it came to rest on her face. A smirk tugged at the corner of his full lips. "Muck the stalls before you came to town?"

She snatched her hand back, her face burning. "I beg your pardon! Just who do you think you are?"

The cad lifted a brow and swept his gaze over her again, amusement in his dark eyes. "I'm a man looking at a beautiful woman dressed like a cowhand."

She stiffened at the rudeness of the remark. Before she could think of a retort, Sheriff Dalton grabbed Jack by the back of his collar and whipped him around.

"Don't worry, Miss Gentry," the sheriff said. "These two drunken yay-hoos will spend time behind bars. Maybe quite a bit of time, once I find out how much damage they've done to the Golden Eagle." He shouted to the crowd. "Okay, let's break it up, folks. The show's over." Some of the bystanders scattered, but most stayed put.

The door to Doctor O'Brien's office opened. Rusty and Doc stepped onto the boardwalk.

Sheriff Dalton turned Jack and Caleb toward the jail, but Jack broke away and snatched his hat from the ground. He slapped it against his leg, sending up a cloud of dust. The late afternoon sun glinted off the hatband of silver conchos as he eased it back onto his head.

Evangeline found her tongue and shouted, "Sheriff, if I were you, I'd keep that man behind bars until hell freezes over!"

"If a woman of mine went to town dressed the way you are, I'd spank her and put her in a dress," Jack yelled over his shoulder, loud enough for all to hear.

Titters came from the crowd.

Evangeline cringed. She grabbed a rock from the street and drew back her arm, but Rusty caught her wrist before she could fling it.

"Oh, no you don't, Miss Eva. He ain't worth it. Besides, you might miss and hit the sheriff."

She squeezed the rock tighter, then relaxed her hand and dropped it. "Come on, Rusty." She scowled. "Let's get you home to your wife."

They climbed onto the buckboard and rumbled south down Main Street. She turned the wagon east onto Noland Road just as Reverend Ingram entered the jailhouse. "Hmm. Looks like the reverend has already heard about the saloon brawl. He should wait until tomorrow to talk to those rowdies. I don't know how he does it."

"Well, that's the business he's in, Miss Eva. Ain't that what the good book says? Love your brother as yourself."

"Yes, I know, Rusty. But in my opinion, the sheriff ought to pack them into the next cattle car headed west and send them on their way."

Rusty gave her a sideways glance. "Boy, that feller sure got on your bad side, didn't he? I've never known you to be this hard on saddle tramps passing through Independence."

She stiffened her back. "He's no saddle tramp. He's a gambler, probably off a riverboat. Did you see how he dressed? I'll bet he spent more on those clothes than I've spent on my entire wardrobe."

Rusty nodded. "He *was* dressed fancy."

She frowned. "He's a gambler all right—a rude and arrogant gambler. That's one face I'm glad I'll never have to see again."

~

Evangeline and Rusty rolled east toward the Gentry ranch on the banks of the Little Blue River. The warm spring sun hung low as dusk approached. Wildflowers dotted the roadside – Purple Thistle, Queen Anne's Lace, and Sweet William. She spotted a cluster of yellow coneflowers blooming in the glade and made a mental note of their location. She'd want to harvest them for her herb supply once they matured.

"Rusty, I remember when Jared and I rode down this hill and I saw our little ranch for the first time. We only had a small herd of quarter horses and a few mustangs then, and Jared had already built a horse barn before he sent for me." She chuckled at the memory. "We lived in a tent for almost a month while the house was being built. The horses had better shelter than we did."

Rusty attempted a smile and rubbed his injured shoulder.

"Yeah, I remember that. Me and Jared had been working day and night to get that barn up before he brought you and the horses out here." His smile faded and sadness touched his eyes. "Jared's passing left a powerful big hole in my heart." He turned to her and quickly added, "I know it ain't nothing compared to the heartache you suffered, Miss Eva."

She patted his hand. "It's okay, Rusty. I still miss Jared, too. It's been three years since he died, and I still miss him every day." She gazed out over the wooded roadside. "But I have to find a way to make peace with the idea of being a widow. I need to find a way to go on alone."

"You know, by rights, I should call you Mrs. Gentry. I'm too danged lazy to spit all that out every time I speak to you."

She laughed. "We've been friends for so long, so you go right on calling me whatever feels right to you. Miss Eva is fine with me."

The buckboard rattled down Little Blue Hill. At the

bottom, she turned into the lane with its overarching oaks leading to her modest house. The setting sun was a huge orange ball on the horizon as they pulled into Evangeline's backyard.

Rachel, a raven-haired young woman, opened the screen door and stepped out onto the porch to greet her husband and boss. She tossed a dishtowel over her shoulder and hurried down the stairs. "Are you all right, my husband?" She reached up and took his hand. "Oh, my goodness, you're all wrapped up! Is it broken?"

"Nah, Doc says it's dislocated. I just need a few days to heal up, and I'll be good as new." He stepped gingerly down from the wagon.

Evangeline turned an unwavering eye on him. "Doc says you can't use that arm at all for a couple of weeks, and you're to heed his advice." She hopped to the ground with considerably more energy than Rusty had.

"The hands have already gone home for the night," Rachel said. She put an arm around her husband's waist as the three of them started up the back steps. "Supper's ready and waiting. *Tamales* and *frijoles* tonight."

Rachel helped Rusty into Evangeline's big kitchen filled with the aroma of spicy beans and steaming coffee. A single lamp flickered in the center of a round oak table, making wavy, crazy-quilt patterns on the whitewashed walls.

Rusty sank into a chair and heaved a sigh. "Man, what a day it's been. And the worst part is, there's a month's worth of repairs waiting to be done to the barns and outbuildings, but now I'm gimpy." A scowl crossed his suntanned face.

Rachel poured steaming coffee into their mugs. "I know, *querida*, but it will be okay. You must look out for yourself right now and get better."

Evangeline nodded. "I'm sure we will find a way to get the work done." She looked down at her hands and fisted them in determination. "I'll bet if you give me instructions, I can finish that roof, myself."

Rusty's eyes shot wide open, and he nearly jumped out of his chair. "You'll do no such thing, Miss Eva! I'll think of something. Don't you worry about that."

~

Evangeline's shoulders slumped with fatigue as Rachel served supper. She'd already put in a full day's work before Rusty fell off the hay barn roof and needed driving into town.

She yawned and stretched her legs under the table, pushing one boot off with the toe of the other. She looked down at the clump of dried mud they left on the floor. That gambler in town had remarked on the way she was dressed. With a stab of her fork, she attacked her tamale. If that pickled polecat thought a woman could run a ranch in lace and crinoline, he had another think coming. What would a fancy-dressed gambler know about hard ranch work, anyway?

And, more importantly, why do I care?

She shook her head to clear her thoughts. "Maybe I'll go back into town tomorrow morning and see if I can find another part-time hand to help out until you're better."

Rusty nodded. "That barn needs roofing right away. We've got plenty of rain ahead of us this spring, and the hay will spoil if it gets soaked. Talk to Reverend Ingram. He might know a good, trustworthy feller to help out for a couple of weeks."

"That's a good idea." She blew into her hot coffee and took a sip. "I'll pick up a few supplies while I'm there, too."

With supper over and the dishes washed, Rusty and Rachel retired to their little cabin a few hundred yards behind the main house. Evangeline lit a candle and blew out the lamp on the kitchen table. She looked out the window over the sink. The breeze had picked up since sunset. It whooshed through the treetops making her wonder if it would rain.

On her way to the bedroom, she passed the two vacant rooms that she'd expected would have noisy children in them by this time in her life. She sighed and pushed the images from her mind. Maybe it wasn't meant to be. Taking care of this place was a full-time job, even with Rusty and the other hired hands. Best not to even think about children and things that might have been.

Evangeline undressed and tossed her dirty work clothes into the floor of the chifforobe. As she brushed her hair, loneliness swept over her. Jared had been dead for more than three years, and she hadn't even considered finding another husband.

She slid into bed and pulled up the covers. When the wind ruffled the leaves outside her window, she reached over and raised it a few inches to allow the cool breeze into her room. They used to lie in bed and talk over the events of the day and plan their future. She missed that, but those days were gone.

Tonight, as she did every night, she whispered a prayer asking the Lord to take care of her needs and protect her family and friends. And she always added a request that someday she might have children of her own.

Her thoughts drifted to the tall gambler. He'd called her beautiful and insulted her in the same breath. What a cad. What a handsome, dark-eyed cad.

She yawned and plumped her pillow. No matter. She had bigger things to worry about. Tomorrow she'd go into town and ask Reverend Ingram to recommend a temporary ranch hand to cover for Rusty while he mended. And that fancy-dressed gambler would still be cooling his heels behind Sheriff Dalton's bars.

Chapter Two

Evangeline struggled to break through the fog of deep sleep. She heard it again. Chester barked and yelped as if trying to raise the dead. Heart thumping, she sat straight up and yanked back the bedside curtain. The pink-tinged sky gave meager light as she scanned the yard for the cause of her dog's agitation.

"I hope it's not that wildcat again." She threw back the covers, rummaged in the dim light for her wrapper, and stumbled out of bed. Robe flying behind her, she raced barefoot to the back door.

Through the window, she saw that Chester jumped and scratched at the door of the smokehouse. Evangeline picked up the shotgun she kept in the corner of the kitchen, checked the loads, then hurried outside.

Chester moved back from his cornered prey and looked at Evangeline as if to say, "Don't worry, I've got it trapped for you." She pulled back both hammers on the shotgun and raised it to her shoulder.

A loud thump, followed by a muffled voice, came from inside.

"Okay, whoever's in there, come out slowly."

She waited. Chester paced and whined, impatient to get at the intruder.

"I said come out now!" she shouted. "I've got a double-barrel shotgun aimed right at you."

The door squeaked open and a child's voice said, "Don't shoot me, ma'am. I'm coming out."

A grimy hand gripped the doorframe. A ragged boot with the sole flapping loose emerged, followed by a head covered with pale blond hair. A boy of about seven or eight years appeared before her. Chester pounced on him, but not in anger as she'd expected. He leaped up and put both forepaws on the boy's chest, his tail wagging.

Stunned, she lowered the gun. "What the...who are you, young man, and what are you doing in my smokehouse at the crack of dawn?"

The boy stood with his head lowered, shoulders drooping. At her question, he looked up at her through the bluest eyes she'd ever seen. She didn't know whether to load him into her wagon and haul him straight to Sheriff Dalton, or take him into the kitchen and feed him.

She took in the sight of him. He wore ragged boots, at least a size too big, patched homespun pants, a size too small, and a dingy white shirt with a button missing. His hair was dirty and needed cutting. Evangeline's heart clenched at his tattered appearance.

"I asked your name and what you're doing pilfering through my smokehouse," she repeated in a tone she hoped sounded stern.

"Yes, ma'am." He gulped and tried again. "My name is Noah Sutton." He peered at her shyly. "And I was stealing food from your smokehouse. That's what I was doing." He patted the shaggy, brown dog and hung his head.

Evangeline put a fisted hand on her hip. "So, you admit it? You admit you were stealing from me."

"Yes, ma'am."

"Don't you know it's wrong to steal, Noah Sutton? And what are you doing running around the countryside before daybreak?"

Before Evangeline could ask any more questions, Rusty hurried down the path from his cabin, followed by Rachel. "What the dickens is going on out here? I heard that dog going crazy, but it took me so long to get my pants on with this lame shoulder, I thought you'd of done shot something by the time I got here."

He caught sight of the tow-headed boy who stood in front of the smokehouse. Then he scratched his stubbly chin and sniffed. "Well, well, well. Who've we got here?" He eyed the boy with curiosity.

"This is Noah Sutton. Chester had him trapped in the smokehouse, although you couldn't tell by the way he's acting now." Evangeline focused her attention on the boy again. "I don't recognize you, Noah. Who are your folks? I'm sure they'll be ashamed when they find out what you've been up to."

"Well, I ain't from around here, ma'am. My family's camped down the river not far from here. I'm sorry I had to break into your smokehouse. I would've shot a rabbit or squirrel, but we're out of shells for my grandpa's rifle. Since he died and Ma's been so sick, we ain't had much to eat." The boy, near fainting, swayed on his feet.

Evangeline leaned her gun against the side of the smokehouse and took him by one stick-thin arm. "Get over there and sit down on that tree stump while I think about this for a minute."

Noah sat, as instructed. Chester lay at his feet, tail thumping the ground.

"Now start this story from the beginning," she said more patiently. "Who, exactly, is camped at the river? And why are you the one looking for food? Aren't there any adults to do the hunting?"

"No, ma'am, there ain't. Gramps died about two weeks ago and my ma's got the same sickness that killed him. Carrie's just a baby, too little to hunt. We was movin' east to a town called Hermann when my Gramps took sick, and we've been camped at the river ever since."

The sun's first rays topped the trees, so she could see him clearly now. She cupped Noah's chin and lifted his face to get a better look at him. His steady gaze showed no deceit.

Rusty hadn't taken his eyes off Noah since he and Rachel arrived. He ran a hand through his wild shock of reddish hair. "Maybe I'd best go check this out and see if he's telling the truth."

Rachel stepped closer to Noah. "My word, Rusty. Anyone can see he has not been eating regularly."

Evangeline shook her head. "No, I'll go myself. He said his mother and a baby are camped at the river. They'll need help fast." Absentmindedly, she wrapped an arm around Noah's shoulder and pulled him close to her side.

"Miss Eva, there ain't no way I'll let you go down there alone." Rusty jutted his chin. "You don't know what you might ride into. It might be dangerous. I'm going with you." Rusty took Noah by the arm and tried to pull him away from Evangeline, but the boy wrapped his arms around her waist and held on.

"No, I'm a grown woman, Rusty, and you're in no shape to ride. I'll deal with this myself. Besides, I need you here to supervise Zeke and Charlie when they come in."

"Please, Evangeline." Rachel's voice rose with worry. "Let Rusty go. He's right. It is not safe for a woman to ride into some strange campsite."

"Don't worry, I'll be fine." Evangeline pulled Noah closer. "Rachel, would you give this boy something to eat? Go easy…it looks like he's been hungry for a while. I don't think his stomach can take anything heavy. And pack some food for me to take along with me."

Rachel sighed and shook her head. "Evangeline Gentry, we have worked for you for over five years and you get more stubborn with every passing year."

"Don't worry. This is my responsibility. I'll be careful, I promise." She picked up her shotgun and hurried into the house to get dressed.

~

Jack jolted straight up in his cot. His eyes flashed wide open. Slowly, his foggy brain took in his surroundings. He turned burning eyes toward the offensive noise as pain shot through his head. Bars. A loud man with a badge on his chest. He seemed to be in jail.

Sheriff Dalton banged on the bars of his cell again with an empty tin cup. "Wake up, gambler, if you want breakfast. Janie from the cafe will be back here in half an hour to pick up these dishes, and she'll take 'em whether you're finished or not."

Jack wilted down onto his cot and shut his eyes again as the blazing light from the window hit him. He threw one arm over his eyes and slapped a hand to his aching head. "Arrgh, stop that infernal racket! Are you trying to kill me?"

"Nope. I think you were trying to do that yourself yesterday afternoon when you went flying through that window at the saloon."

"Oh, yes. The saloon." Jack sat up slower than an old man and rubbed the lump on his head. The sheriff unlocked the cell. He set a plate of eggs, bacon, and hot buttered biscuits next to him on the cot, slammed the door, and then hung the key back on its peg.

Sheriff Dalton, a middle-aged man short but built like a bull, walked across the room to the pot-bellied stove. His thick, luxurious handlebar mustache curled on the ends, a stark contrast to the lack of hair on his head. The sheriff brought over a cup of black coffee that smelled strong enough to strip paint from the walls and handed it through the bars.

Jack sipped the hot brew and rubbed his bleary eyes. "Sheriff, some of yesterday's events are, uh, still a bit sketchy to me." He touched the knot on his head again. "It feels like somebody broke a chair over my head. Maybe you'd be kind enough to tell me what I'm doing in jail?"

Sheriff Dalton gave an ornery little laugh. He sipped the last of his coffee and leaned against the windowsill near his desk. "Well, now, let me see if I can help you out here. Seems like you and young Caleb

Hutchison had a bit of a disagreement over at the Golden Eagle Saloon. You got into a fistfight. When the barkeep suggested you take the fight outside, you thought he meant you should go by way of the big plate glass window." He chuckled again, seeming to enjoy his own sense of humor.

"Next thing I knew you were in a heap at the feet of Miss Gentry, making insulting remarks to that fine young woman – one of our town's leading ladies, I might add." He banged his coffee cup on the desk.

Jack cringed at the noise, and then snapped his eyes open as recollection swept over him. "That woman? The one in men's clothes and muddy boots?" He wrinkled his nose in distaste.

The sheriff slammed a ham-sized fist into his other palm. "Now you better watch yourself, mister. That's a highly respected member of our community you're talking about. She's a lady. It ain't her fault she has to run that ranch all but single-handed."

An aroma of bacon penetrated Jack's muddled brain, so he took a slice and dipped it in his egg yolk. "Well, you may be right, but as near as I can remember, she was about to hurl a rock at my head as you dragged me off to jail." He popped the bite into his mouth. Jack laid his plate aside and inspected his sore arm. He grimaced as he rolled up his shirt sleeve and examined the wound.

"By the way," Sheriff Dalton asked, "how'd you get your arm winged like that? I haven't had a telegram telling me to be on the lookout for any bank robbers coming my way."

"I'm no bank robber. Just had a slight disagreement with a man back in St. Louie after I had the better poker hand." Satisfied with his examination, Jack returned his attention to his breakfast.

"Maybe I'd better get Doc over here to take a look at that arm of yours. I don't want anybody to die of blood poisoning here in my jail."

"It's only a flesh wound. I've been dousing it with whiskey so it doesn't get infected."

"And I'm sure you've had no short supply of that stuff."

Jack furrowed his brow. "Now that you mention it, my supply was getting low." He held out his coffee cup. "Got anything to sweeten this swamp water? A shot of Irish whiskey might help."

The door opened and a slender, middle-aged man stepped into the office.

"Morning, Reverend Ingram," Sheriff Dalton greeted him.

"Good morning, Sheriff."

The parson closed the door behind him and crossed the room, a broad smile on his pleasant face.

Sheriff Dalton grabbed the coffee pot and poured a cup for Reverend Ingram without asking if he wanted one. "I'll bet you're here to have a word with our young gambler, ain't you?"

"Why, yes, as a matter of fact, I am." Reverend Ingram scrutinized Jack through the bars of his cell. "I always like to pay a visit to the wayward young fellows who end up incarcerated in our town. I dropped by to see you yesterday evening, but you were asleep—"

"Passed out," the sheriff mumbled.

"If you don't mind talking while I eat, come on in and sit down." Jack patted the spot next to him on the cot.

Sheriff Dalton took the keys from their peg on the wall, handed the reverend his cup of coffee, and unlocked the door. "I figure you're wasting your time. But I reckon it's your job." The door clanged shut behind the reverend. "Now you mind your manners in there, gambler."

Jack stopped mid-motion, fork halfway to his mouth. He started to ask the sheriff why he kept calling him "gambler," when it dawned on him that somewhere, he had saddlebags holding thousands of dollars. "By the way, Sheriff, where are my belongings?"

"Oh, you mean that fancy concho hat of yours? It's locked up in the back room."

"And my saddlebags?"

"They're with your hat and gun. Why? Do you think we're a bunch of thieves here in this town?"

"No, no, not at all. I just wanted to be sure they weren't left behind at the saloon," he said, not wanting to incur the sheriff's wrath.

Reverend Ingram cleared his throat and patted the Bible. "Speaking of guns, saloons, and strong drink. Young man, I wonder if you've given any thought to where your life is headed? You seem like an intelligent fellow. Have you ever considered that the path you're on leads only to destruction? Your being here in jail right now provides a perfect example of that." The reverend paused and his tone became pensive. "This time it's just the jailhouse in Independence, Missouri, but next time you could find yourself in the Federal Prison in Leavenworth."

Jack wiped his plate with the last of his biscuit and

looked at the pastor, trying not to show his increasing irritation. "Reverend, I know you're here doing what you think is best, but right now, I've got a headache the size of Texas, and all I want is to pay my fine and be on my way. I promise I'll stop by the church and have a good talk with the Lord before I leave town."

"Ah, ah, ah. Not so fast there." Sheriff Dalton spoke through the cell bars. "Joe over at the Golden Eagle says you and young Hutchison owe him fifty dollars for damages. Hutchison's already paid what he owes. If you can come up with your part, and enough to pay your fine, then you can go on your way."

Jack swallowed the biscuit and washed it down with the last of his bitter coffee. He made a disgusted face. "That'll be no problem at all, Sheriff. If you'll bring me my saddlebags, I'll pay up and be out of town by noon."

Sheriff Dalton took another set of keys from his desk drawer and clomped to the storage room. Moments later, he reappeared, opened the cell door, and tossed Jack's saddlebags to him. Jack caught the limp bags effortlessly.

His jaw dropped. He opened them and shoved his hand into each one as if the money might just be hidden somewhere out of sight. "What! What is this? Where's the money I had in these saddlebags?" His rant shot a wave of nauseating pain through his head. "These bags had money in them. Lots of money. Gold and paper!"

Sheriff Dalton's face reddened. "Now, what are you implying, gambler? You think I stole your money?"

"No, I didn't say you stole my money, but *somebody* did! Where were these bags when you got them? Were they in the saloon? Who gave them to you?"

"Joe at the saloon gave me the bags and your gun when I went to talk to him about the damages. But if you're gonna accuse Joe of stealing, you're dead wrong. Joe ain't no thief either."

Jack jumped up and grabbed the bars of his cell. "Somebody stole the money from my saddle bags. It's gone! Over five thousand dollars!" He thundered at Sheriff Dalton. Jack rattled the bars in his clenched hands. "What are you going to do about it, Sheriff?"

"Don't worry about it, gambler. I'll do some asking around at the saloon. You just settle down."

Jack held his head in his hands and groaned. "Unbelievable. Just unbelievable. There goes my entry fee for the poker tournament. There goes my gambling palace." He slowly raised his head and met the preacher's eyes. "Well, Reverend, maybe you're right about the gambling life. It sure isn't paying off for me right now."

Sheriff Dalton nodded in agreement. He took a toothpick from his pocket, stuck it in the corner of his mouth, and walked back to his desk. "Yep, it sure looks that way. Seems you and me will be keeping company for at least thirty days."

Chapter Three

Evangeline saddled her mare, Scarlett, and pulled Noah up behind her. Over the saddle horn, she hung a bag containing beans, a slab of bacon, and cornmeal, along with some of the previous night's leftovers. She nudged Scarlett's sides and turned her toward the Little Blue River. "Okay, Noah, where is this campsite of your family's?"

"Just over that ridge and south a bit."

They followed the river for about a mile until it took a sharp turn to the south.

"There it is." Noah pointed to a canvas tent under the shade of an oak tree that stood in a clearing about a hundred yards from the riverbank.

The tent sagged as if it might topple with one good gust of wind. Outside, a cold firepit and a wagon with sparse belongings gave the camp a forlorn look. A few items of clothing hung on low tree branches.

She rode up and helloed the camp. "Mrs. Sutton, you in there? I'm Evangeline Gentry. I found your son in my smokehouse this morning." There was no reply. After a minute, she called again.

"Mrs. Sutton?"

Faint coughing came from inside the tent and a baby's cry was barely audible. "Jump down, Noah." She dismounted after him. "Please wait out here until I call for you."

Evangeline approached the tent with caution and pulled back the flap. Inside, the air reeked of sickness. The stench of stale sweat, dirty diapers, and vomit pervaded the small space. A blond woman lay holding a tiny girl who looked to be a little over a year old.

She ducked inside the tent. "Mrs. Sutton?" She knelt and laid a hand on the young woman's thin shoulder.

Mrs. Sutton turned her face toward Evangeline and looked at her with the same blue eyes as Noah's. "Lady, please take my children out of here." Her voice was a desperate whisper. Mrs. Sutton took Evangeline's hand but was so weak that her hand fell away. "I don't think I'll make it, but my children need a doctor." She coughed, the sound faint and hoarse.

"Let me get you some water." Evangeline glanced around the tent but found only an empty bucket. She ran outside and took her canteen from Scarlett's saddle horn. She tied back the tent flap to allow fresh air and light inside.

Evangeline leaned over the woman's cot. She caught her breath at what she saw. Cyanotic skin. There was blood coming from her nostrils and at the corner of her mouth. Influenza. *Lord, please help the poor woman.* From the looks of things, the baby had it, too. No doubt, it was what had killed their grandfather. She knelt beside Mrs. Sutton and held the canteen to her parched lips. She wet a rag with the cool water and put it to her forehead.

"You'll be fine," she said, even as she observed the woman's weak condition.

"No, I don't think so. Please, get help for my children."

The baby wailed softly, but no tears came from her eyes. There wasn't a minute to waste. Although Noah showed no signs of illness, the baby was sick and probably starving. She lifted the child, cradled her in her arms, and squeezed water from a wet cloth into her tiny mouth. Fear tightened her throat. The baby was so weak she might die in her arms.

She hoped Mrs. Sutton didn't notice how her voice trembled as she spoke. "I'm going to send your son back to my place. We'll get help for all of you." She adjusted the baby in her arms and ducked outside into the fresh air.

"Noah, do exactly as I say. Get on Scarlett and ride back to the ranch. Tell Rachel to have my two ranch hands bring a wagon with plenty of blankets right away. Then tell her to go into town and get Doc as fast as she can. Can you remember all that?"

"Yes, ma'am, I can. Is my ma okay?"

"Let's give Doc a chance to look at her, dear. Hurry—get going!"

Noah scrambled onto Scarlett's back and kicked her sides.

Evangeline gently nestled the baby into a blanket in the back of the old wagon and tiptoed inside to Mrs. Sutton. She covered her mouth with her shirttail, knowing it would do nothing to keep her from getting sick. She moistened the cloth again with cool water, dabbed Mrs. Sutton's warm face, and then crept under the tent flap to tend to the baby.

This meant Rusty, and Rachel had been exposed to influenza. Soon Zeke and Charlie would be here, too. She sat down on the tailgate of the wagon. She'd nursed the sick before but never faced a situation like this one. How should she handle it? If she took this family to town, she'd expose the whole town. She couldn't leave them here sick and in squalor. She'd have to take them back to her ranch and let Doc O'Brien treat them there.

Before long, the sound of the big buckboard lumbering down the side of the hill alerted her to her ranch hands' arrival. She ran toward them and shouted, "Stop right there, Charlie! Leave the buckboard and you and Zeke go back to the house. These people have influenza. Don't come into the camp. Go back to the ranch, saddle up and go on home until we know how bad things are here."

From behind the wagon came a voice with a familiar twang. "Yep, you boys go on home. We can handle things here." Rusty rode around the side of the wagon and into camp, scanning his surroundings.

"Rusty Cunningham, if you aren't the most stubborn, hardheaded mule of a man I've ever seen in my entire life. Do you know what you're doing? Putting yourself and Rachel in real danger by being here. I think this family has the grippe."

"There ain't no way you can handle it all by yourself, Miss Eva. Besides, me and Rachel have already had it. Just step aside and let me get these young'uns and their ma into the wagon."

Evangeline grabbed him by the shirt sleeve and pulled him aside. "She's bad, Rusty. I don't think their ma's going to live. You need to go back and take Rachel away from the house. I'm taking this family home with me." She looked back at the tent. "I just hope Mrs. Sutton makes it that far."

Rusty set his stubborn jaw. "Like I said, me and Rachel have both had the grippe. Here's what I'll do. I'll stay here with the lady. I think Doc needs to see these young'uns first, especially that baby. After he looks 'em over, send him out here to see about their ma."

Evangeline sighed. "I guess that is the best solution." She picked up the baby and walked to Noah, who stood nearby in stunned silence.

"Noah, get in the bed of the wagon," she said, her voice gentle. He did as she instructed, and Evangeline put the baby into his arms. When a tear trickled down his smudged cheek, she reached down and squeezed his shoulders.

Evangeline tied Scarlett to the tailgate before turning and handing her canteen to Rusty.

"What about my ma?" Noah asked, choking on a sob.

She touched his cheek. "Rusty is staying with your ma, Noah. I'll explain things to you as soon as we get home."

Chapter Four

Rachel Rios Cunningham galloped into Independence in a cloud of dust. She stopped in front of Doc O'Brien's office, tied her horse to the hitching post, and burst through the door.

Doc looked up from his newspaper, his eyebrows knit together over his spectacles. "What is it, Rachel? Has Rusty taken a turn for the worse?"

Rachel stood in the doorway, breathless. "No, it isn't Rusty. Miss Gentry asked me to come for you. She found a family camped down by the river this morning, all of them sick. She says it's influenza and wants you to come as quickly as you can."

Doc folded his newspaper and slowly rubbed his hands over his face. The chair groaned in resistance as he heaved himself up. "I'll get my bag."

He retrieved several bottles from the cabinet and placed them into a medical bag as old and worn as the man, himself.

"Rachel, I saw the reverend and his wife going into the cafe. Tell him what's going on. He'll want to make a trip out to Evangeline's later, but tell him to spread the word—nobody else is to come out there until I say so."

~

Rachel locked gazes with Mrs. Ingram.

"She's doing what?" Mrs. Ingram's mouth formed a perfect little O shape. She threw a hand across her ample bosom. "Oh, my word, Elias, did you hear that? Evangeline has taken in a family with influenza!" Wide-eyed, she shifted her gaze from her husband to Rachel. "Well, there's nothing to do but go out there and help her take care of them. It's our duty, Elias. That's all there is to it."

Despite the gravity of the situation, Rachel almost giggled. The difference in their appearance and personalities was striking. The reverend was slight of build, soft-spoken and mild-mannered. Tall and stout, Mrs. Ingram held a commanding presence.

"Tell Evangeline we'll come as soon as we can, Rachel," the reverend said. "We'll give Doctor O'Brien a chance to examine the family, then we'll go out and offer our help."

"Thank you, Reverend, I will let her know." Rachel turned to leave, then remembered her other task. "Oh, and I know this is not the time but, Rusty took a fall roofing the barn yesterday and dislocated his shoulder. He won't be able to do much for at least a couple of weeks, and Miss Gentry wants to hire a man to finish the repair. Can you recommend someone, Padre?"

He lowered his fork to the table and patted the corner of his mouth with a napkin. He stared into space while he mulled it over. "Well, now let me see. Not right offhand, I can't but..." His eyes lit up, and he tossed his napkin on the table. "I just might know someone. Let me speak to him. If everything works out, Sarah and I will bring him with us later when we come out to the ranch."

~

Jack leaned against the bars of the jailhouse window, overlooking the back alley. He held his aching head, tormented by his thoughts. *Who took that money from my saddlebags? I still think it was that barkeep. Or at least I bet he knows who did. Somebody saw something. Everything depends on that money, my entire future.*

Jack blew out a long breath and sat on his cot. The odds of finding who took his money were slim. Getting any of it back after thirty days in jail would be next to impossible. He had to get out of here and find that money, or he'd miss the tournament in San Francisco. Without those winnings, it could take years before he accumulated enough money to build his gambling palace.

The front door of the jail opened. Reverend Ingram walked in with a placid smile.

"Back so soon, Reverend?" Sheriff Dalton moved to take the keys from their peg to open the cell door, but the reverend stopped him.

"You're the one I want to talk to, Owen. Would you mind stepping outside with me for a moment?"

The sheriff shrugged and hung the keys back on the peg. "Sure, Reverend."

The sheriff closed the door behind them, but the murmur of their voices still reached Jack. Sheriff

Dalton's voice rose in excitement from time to time. The reverend spoke in a calm tone, as if in an attempt to placate and reason with the sheriff. Before long, the two men re-entered the office. Sheriff Dalton lumbered across the room, jerked his desk drawer open, and extracted the same set of keys he'd taken out earlier that morning.

Soon, he emerged from the storeroom with Jack's saddlebags, hat, and gun in hand. He opened the cell and tossed Jack's belongings onto the cot. "Okay, Brannigan, the reverend has talked me into releasing you into his custody for thirty days."

Jack sat bolt upright and smiled first at the reverend, then looked at the sheriff.

"Don't get too excited, son. There's a couple of stipulations to this here arrangement."

Reverend Ingram nodded. "Yes, that's right. You'll have to do service for the community—make yourself useful for the next thirty days."

Jack laughed and leaned back on the cot again.

Sheriff Dalton continued. "Now, since the circuit judge won't be in town for another two weeks, I'm the one to make the decision about this. If you—"

"Service for the community? What's that all about? You'll have me sweeping boardwalks and cleaning outhouses?"

Sheriff Dalton snorted and tugged the corner of his mustache. "I like those ideas better than the reverend's, but he's got something else in mind. If you give me your word you'll do exactly as the reverend tells you, I'll release you into his custody. If you leave town, I'll have a posse on your trail faster'n you can jingle your spurs."

"Well, what do you think, Mr. Brannigan?" The reverend's gray eyes were hopeful. "Will you go along with my idea?"

Jack stood and flashed a smile as he eased his hat into place. "I don't wear spurs but, sure, I'll go along with it."

Sheriff Dalton shook his head. A frown creased his brow. "I'm still not crazy about this idea, but since Miss Gentry needs help so much right now, I'll go along with it. For her sake."

Jack balked. "Miss Gentry? You mean the woman from yesterday with the pants and the boots?"

Reverend Ingram stepped into the cell, put a hand on Jack's shoulder, and propelled him toward the door. "Get your belongings and come along, young fellow. We have some talking to do."

Jack followed the preacher out the door and sucked in a deep breath of fresh air. "I could use a hair of the dog that bit me," he said as he looked down Main Street toward the saloon. He really wanted to nail the bartender to the wall and find out what happened to his money.

Reverend Ingram chuckled and grabbed Jack by his arm. "I think the cafe's a better idea. Or we can go to the church if you prefer."

They stepped into the street. "The cafe will do, but since somebody has emptied my saddlebags of all my money, I can't even buy myself a cup of coffee."

The reverend patted him on the back. "Don't worry, son. I'll pay for your coffee."

They stepped into the dusty street, and Jack turned a longing eye toward the saloon. He desperately wanted to have a little talk with that barkeep.

Stepping onto the wooden sidewalk, Reverend Ingram opened the door to the cafe and made a sweeping motion with his hand. "After you, son."

Jack sank into a chair, narrowed his eyes at the reverend, and drummed his fingertips on the table. Before he could ask any of his numerous questions, a young waitress sidled up to their table. She gazed down at Jack, eyelashes fluttering. "I've never seen you around town, mister. I'm sure I would have remembered. What can I get for you?" She smiled and swayed her hips.

Jack gave the reverend a sheepish grin. "I think we both want coffee."

"Yes, coffee and bring us each a piece of Janie's strawberry pie, would you, Corrine?" He turned back to Jack, seemingly oblivious to the waitress's flirtation. "Best pie in town."

Jack watched Corrine sashay her way back into the kitchen, craning his neck to see around the couple sitting at the next table. Then, he returned his attention to the reverend.

"Now, Padre. Tell me all about this community service. And what does the cranky Miss Gentry have to do with it?"

"Ah, yes, the community service. Well, Mr. Brannigan, it's quite simple. Since you can't pay your fine, you owe this town thirty days. You can serve it sitting in jail if you prefer, or you can serve it in a way that benefits others."

Corrine sat their pie in front of them and then filled both cups with coffee. If the reverend noticed Jack's slice of pie was twice the size of his, he didn't say a word. He studied Jack as he sipped his coffee.

"I'd guess a young man like you would rather stay busy in the sunshine, rather than stare at brick walls and bars. Miss Gentry has a little ranch out east of town. Her foreman got himself hurt yesterday. She needs a man to take his place until he's able to work again. Are you handy with anything besides a deck of cards?"

Jack stuck a fork into the warm pie and crooked the corner of his mouth. "I wasn't born in a saloon."

"Well, that's wonderful, son. You'll feel better about yourself after a day of hard work, especially knowing you've helped a nice lady like Miss Gentry."

To avoid saying something snippy, Jack stuffed pie into his mouth. "I'll stay at the Gentry place, I suppose?"

"We haven't worked out the details yet, but I'd reckon she'll put you up in the barn, or one of her outbuildings. Either way, I'll come out often to check on you."

Jack straightened his shoulders like a soldier about to march into battle and took a deep breath. *Whatever it takes to stay out of jail. Whatever it takes to find my money and get to San Francisco.*

The reverend cleared his throat and set his cup down. "One more thing. It seems Miss Gentry has taken a small family into her home. They're all sick—most likely with influenza."

Jack dropped his fork onto the blue-checkered tablecloth and leaned forward. A burst of laughter escaped his lips. "You're making me perform this 'community service' at a ranch full of people with the grippe?"

The reverend shrugged and nodded. He gave Jack an innocent smile. "Mr. Brannigan, you don't have to do this. You can go back and serve your time in jail, but this option is open if you want it. The way I see it, if you sleep in the barn, there's no reason you'd come in contact with those in the main house."

Jack threw up his hands in defeat. "Oh, I'd rather take my chances with influenza, Reverend. When do I start?"

"Right away." He looked down at his plate and quickly added, "Oh, and by the way, I'll expect you in church every Sunday."

Jack froze, his mouth open, awaiting a fork full of pie. The crease around his lips tightened, and he lowered his fork. "Is that so? Since when is it lawful to force a man to go to church?" He clenched his teeth so hard they should have shattered. "The church might be struck by lightning when I walk through the doors, but if you insist." He steepled his fingers, then folded them tight.

Reverend Ingram gave him a wink. "I consider it part of my rehabilitation program."

Chapter Five

Evangeline moved the pillows to the sides of the bed and laid the blond baby girl between them. A knock sounded at the front door. She peeked through the window to see Doc O'Brien's buggy in the yard. "Come on in, Doc." She closed the door behind him. "Thank you for getting here so fast."

The portly man shuffled into the bedroom and bent over the child to start his examination.

Evangeline moved to the side of the bed and worried the cuff of one sleeve. "Her name is Carrie. Both she and her mother are feverish and dehydrated. The boy has no symptoms that I've noticed, but I'm afraid for this baby."

Doc pulled up a chair, removed a thermometer and stethoscope from his bag, and set to work. He pressed the baby's abdomen and checked for cyanosis and blood in her nostrils.

"Get cool water to bathe her, Evangeline, and make broth." Doc's tone was grim. "This baby's mighty dehydrated and malnourished. I don't think she can stomach anything solid. I suspect the whole family hasn't eaten in a while."

She returned with a basin of water and set it on the table beside the bed. She opened both windows to get a cross breeze into the room. "What do you think, Doc? Is it the grippe?"

Doc placed his stethoscope back into his bag and nodded. "Yes, it is. I'll take a look at the boy before I go out to examine their mother, but chances are if he were going to contract the disease, he'd have it by now. From what you've told me, the mother has entered the third and final stage."

Evangeline moistened a cloth with cool water and pressed it to Carrie's forehead. "I'll take care of these children, Doc. And if Mrs. Sutton's strong enough, you and Rusty bring her here, too."

After Doc examined Noah, he gave Evangeline detailed instructions on how to care for Carrie. Satisfied, he went out to his buggy. "I hope you realize what you've taken upon yourself, young lady. This illness can be deadly so you'll have to quarantine yourself here until all danger has passed. Several of us old-timers have immunity from the epidemic that came through town about ten years ago. The Reverend and Mrs. Ingram both had it, as have I, so we can safely come and go."

"Yes, Rusty said he and Rachel are both immune, too. We'll be fine, Doc." She looked up as he seated himself in his buggy and picked up the reins.

"I'll get down there right away to see about the children's mother. You take care of yourself. I'll come back this evening."

~

39

About lunchtime, the kitchen door opened behind Evangeline. She turned from the pot of soup that simmered on the stove and gazed into Rusty's weary eyes. "Mrs. Sutton? How is she?"

Rusty shook his head and dropped into a chair. "She's gone."

Evangeline laid her wooden spoon on the stove and stared out the window in the direction of the river. Tears stung her eyes as she remembered the young woman lying in a dirty tent, clutching her baby near as she clung to life. She had probably been about Evangeline's age. She'd been on her way to a new place, full of hope for a better life. Now, that dream was over, and she'd left behind two helpless children.

"How will I tell Noah? How do I tell a child he has no family? No father and now no mother."

"It'll be tough, for sure. Why don't you let me and Rachel tell him?"

"No, I can't do that. I brought the children into my home, and I'll be the one taking care of them until they're well. I'll have to find the words to tell Noah about his mother." She stared blankly through the window. "They're orphans now."

~

Evangeline spent the next few hours sponge-bathing Carrie and cutting up old sheets to make diapers. The baby's hair fell in dirty curls about her face.

Evangeline smiled at Carrie. "One day soon, I'm going to give you a proper bath, and then I'm gonna put you in a pretty pink dress and hair ribbons." She rubbed a smudge from Carrie's face. "And your brother Noah rides so well. I think my pony, Blue Smoke would make a good mount for a boy his age."

Evangeline pursed her lips. *Lord, please don't let some family member come asking about the Suttons. I know You sent these children to me because they need loving care, and that's exactly what I can give them.*

She sent Noah to bring in wood, then built a fire. Together, they dragged out the washtub and filled it with buckets of water. She dressed Noah in an old shirt of Jared's, and then scrubbed the children's clothes and hung them on the line to dry.

As the sun sank to the horizon, the reverend and Mrs. Ingram's buggy rattled into the yard, followed by a man on a black stallion. "Thank heavens," Evangeline muttered. "The Ingrams have arrived and they must've found a hired man for me, too." She dried her hands on her apron, tucked a light brown curl into its pins, and hurried out to meet them.

Mrs. Ingram jumped down from the carriage with amazing agility for a woman of her age then bustled over to Evangeline. "Oh, my dear girl." She hugged Evangeline with her usual flourish. "How will you manage things here with only an injured ranch hand and his wife? Let me see those little ones. How many are there?"

Evangeline squeezed her in return. "Two children, Noah and Carrie. The youngest is still a baby. Noah isn't sick, thank heavens, but their mother died, Mrs. Ingram. She passed on right after I took the children. And they lost their grandfather within the last couple of weeks, too."

"Oh, my word." Mrs. Ingram pulled a handkerchief from the bodice of her dress and dabbed at her nose.

The reverend stepped down from the carriage. "That's devastating news, Evangeline." He held out his arms, and she leaned in to kiss his cheek.

As she glanced over the pastor's shoulder, she locked eyes with Black Jack Brannigan. He sat his horse with all the arrogance of a Spanish Conquistador. He wore his hat pushed back casually, dark hair spilling from under the brim. His posture was erect and held the lithe elegance of a panther. His cocky grin told her he knew she wasn't happy to see him. He must have considered it funny.

"Miss Gentry." He leaned forward in a dramatic bow.

Instinctively, Evangeline rolled her eyes.

Reverend Ingram turned to him. "Oh, I beg your pardon. Miss Evangeline Gentry, this is Jack Brannigan. I understand you two have, er, already met."

Jack dismounted and reached her in two long strides. "Allow me to offer my apologies, Miss Gentry. My behavior when we met yesterday was inexcusable. Please forgive me." Despite his apologetic words, his tone declared his lack of sincerity.

She made little attempt to hide her displeasure at seeing him again. "Mr. Brannigan, what can I do for you? I'm sure you've heard that we have influenza here. You should probably get back on your horse and ride off my property as fast as you can go." She forced a smile.

"Oh, Evangeline, Mr. Brannigan is here to help with chores while Rusty mends," Reverend Ingram said. "The sheriff agreed to release him into my custody to serve out his thirty-day sentence. He'll be working here on your ranch. He's going to put the roof on your barn for you."

She looked from Black Jack Brannigan to Reverend Ingram and shook her head. "Oh, no, Reverend. No, no, no. Not this man."

Reverend Ingram looked crestfallen. "But Evangeline, your ranch hands have left, your foreman's injured, and you need a man to reroof your barn."

"I'm sorry, Reverend, but there must be someone else. Anyone else. For goodness' sake, look at him. He's a dandy, a riverboat gambler." She wrinkled her nose in distaste. "What would he know about ranch work?" When she called him a dandy, Jack flinched. *Good. Serves the blackguard right.*

Reverend Ingram ran a finger around the edge of his white collar and shrugged. "Truthfully, Evangeline, there is no one else. Please remember you have a contagious and deadly disease here. Where will I find anyone willing to fill in for Rusty under these circumstances?" He nodded in Jack's direction. "This gentleman has agreed to take his chances with the grippe while he works off his thirty-day obligation to Sheriff Dalton. He'll roof your barn and help with the ranch while Rusty heals."

She huffed and tossed her head. "Forgive me, but this man is going to put a roof on my barn? I doubt he even knows what a hammer looks like."

Jack raised his eyebrows. "Oh, you'd be surprised at the things I know." "I'm a man of many talents and full of surprises." He curled his lips into a bright smile. "And I'll bet you'd like me to get busy on that barn right away."

Evangeline looked him up and down in the same exaggerated manner he'd looked at her the day before. "I suppose you're going to roof my barn dressed like that?"

"Well, these are the only clothes I have, since I was robbed. So, I guess I'll have to do ranch work dressed this way."

Rachel stood at the kitchen window as if hanging on every word. She opened the back door and stepped outside. "He could probably fit into one of Rusty's work shirts. Let me run to the cabin and see what I can find." She shook her head as she descended the steps, muttering something in Spanish.

Evangeline wrinkled her nose. "Yes, and you'd better bring Rusty, too. I'm sure he'll need to give this...gentleman...step-by-step instructions." She turned to the reverend. "It's a long drive back to town every night. Will he stay with you and Mrs. Ingram while he's in your custody?"

The reverend put an arm around her shoulder and guided her toward the house. "I meant to mention that to you, dear. It's too far to travel every evening, so I thought he could stay in the cabin with Rusty and Rachel, or maybe in one of your barns."

Evangeline stopped in her tracks and shook her head forcefully. "Stay here twenty-four hours a day? Now, I don't know about that. Doesn't seem like a good idea to me."

"Oh, the barn will do nicely, Miss Gentry." Jack curled his lips into a teeth-baring sneer. "I can make a bed of straw and gaze up at the stars through the hole in the roof. Then in the morning, I can milk the cows and feed the horses."

"I wouldn't let you anywhere near my horses, but you're welcome to milk the cows if you choose." She scowled and whirled around to Jack. "Well, Mr. Brannigan, it seems I'm stuck with you. Rusty's on light duty and can't chop wood right now. We're getting a little low, so I'll expect to see you over at the woodpile after you finish working on the barn."

He smiled and gritted his teeth. "That'll be no problem."

Mrs. Ingram shook her head and marched past Jack up the steps and into the house.

Evangeline rolled her eyes and huffed. She mounted the steps to the porch. "Mrs. Ingram, I'll take you to the children."

Chapter Six

Jack leaned against a workbench and rolled up the sleeves of Rusty's old shirt. The blue cotton stretched tight as he flexed his shoulders. "A bit snug, but I suppose it'll do."

Rusty glared at him through narrowed eyes but said nothing. He gathered tools for the roofing job and dropped them on a work table. Holding up the hammer, he said, "This is a hammer. You use it to pound these little sharp doo-dads into the wood." He pointed to the nails. "And you'll need this saw to cut boards to replace the rotten wood up there." He pointed to the gaping hole in the roof.

Jack crossed his arms over his broad chest. "Why, thank you... Rusty, is it?" He took the saw from Rusty and touched the saw teeth, testing their sharpness. "You don't take care of your tools very well, do you, Rusty? Looks like you might have left this out in the rain. Is that how you came by your nickname?"

The lanky redhead looked like he might explode. "I most certainly do take care of the tools, mister. I take good care of everything on this ranch, including Miss Evangeline Gentry." He stepped closer and locked eyes with Jack. "You'd do well to remember that, gambler.

I'm the hard case you need to worry about on this here place. And I'll be watching you." Rusty tromped to the door and opened it. "We'd best get started on this. There ain't much daylight left. I figure I'll have to walk you through this repair step by step."

Jack gathered the tools and followed. "Okay, Rusty, where are the lumber and shingles for the roof? And unless you've already measured and cut the boards, I'll need a yardstick. From the looks of those crossbeams, I'll need to replace a couple of those, too, so I hope you have a few two-by-sixes here." As though it were a child's toy, he lifted the ladder and leaned it against the side of the barn. "Well, do you have those two-by-sixes or not?" he asked over his shoulder.

"How does a man like you know so much about roofing?" Rusty threw a hammer against the barn with more force than necessary.

Jack strapped on a nail apron. "A man like me? And just what kind of man do you think I am?"

"I think you're a man that got hisself arrested for barroom brawling and, from what I hear, a man that makes his living gambling."

"Don't worry, I can roof the barn. That is, if you've got the materials I need. Do you have those two-by-sixes or not?" Jack stooped and picked up the saw and hammer.

"You'll find the supplies in the back of the barn behind the old sawhorses. I've got other things to do." Rusty trudged away, then turned around. "I'll come back to check on you later, Brannigan. I reckon you'll need a lot of supervising."

Jack raised his head and looked at Rusty. "Why? Are you afraid I'll fall off the roof and bust my shoulder or something?"

Rusty balled his fists and stomped off toward the house.

Jack chuckled and stepped into the barn.

~

The screen door squeaked as Evangeline pushed it open and stepped out onto the back porch. "Goodnight, Reverend, and thank you for all your help. And you, Mrs. Ingram, what would I have done without you today?" She wrapped her arms around the stout woman and patted her back.

"Not at all, dear. Elias and I will be back around two o'clock tomorrow to do what we can." She took Evangeline by the shoulders, her expression stern. "Now, promise me you'll try to get some rest tonight. And make sure that no-account riverboat gambler does his part. After all, when the sheriff released him into Elias' custody, he stipulated that Mr. Brannigan would do one month of community service. If you don't need his help here, I don't know who does. That's why Elias decided the best way for that impertinent man to do penance would be to help here at your ranch. Most people wouldn't be willing to turn their home into a makeshift hospital as you have." She raised her eyebrows. "You know you'll be under quarantine yourself for the next few weeks."

Evangeline offered a weak smile. "Don't worry, Mrs. Ingram. I'll see to it that Mr. Fancy Pants works those soft gambler's hands until they have calluses."

Mrs. Ingram hooked her arm through her husband's and giggled.

Reverend Ingram spoke more charitably about Black Jack Brannigan. "Evangeline, try to think of this as an opportunity to show Mr. Brannigan the merits of living a godly life. We don't want him to think of this time spent helping you as punishment, but rather as a learning experience." He turned to his wife and gave her a stern look. "And, Sarah, he isn't here to do penance. He's here to do service for the community."

His wife rolled her eyes and huffed.

"Yes, of course, you're right, Reverend." Evangeline folded her arms and stared down at her feet. "And I'm hoping to teach Mr. Brannigan plenty while he's working here on my ranch."

The Reverend and Mrs. Ingram climbed into their buggy and drove down the dusty lane onto the main road.

Evangeline sighed and went back into the kitchen. She was tired. Her back ached from carrying water, washing and hanging clothes, and she'd barely sat down all day. She dried her hands on her apron, swiped a strand of loose hair behind her ears, and started putting away the dinner dishes.

At the sound of Carrie fussing in the bedroom, Evangeline dropped her dishtowel to the table. "Coming, Carrie." She poured a cup of fresh water and hurried to her side. "Here you go, sweetie." She sat Carrie up and stroked the baby's hair as she sipped her water.

Evangeline looked out the window to see a full moon rising in the eastern sky. *Where is that Jack Brannigan? He should have finished working on the barn long ago and been back here helping with other things.*

She picked up the baby, went to the parlor, and sank into a rocking chair. The moon slid from behind the clouds and lit the room, turning the whitewashed walls the color of creamy pearls. It looked to be a long night. Although she was weary and longed for rest, she rocked the baby and began to sing.

T'was in the town, where I was born.
When green buds all were swellin'.
Sweet William on his deathbed lay,
For the love of Barbra Allen.
He sent his servant to the town,
To the place where she was dwellin'.
My master bid ye come to him,
If yer name be Barbra Allen.

"Now, isn't that a depressing song to sing to a sick child?"

Evangeline looked up, startled at the voice coming from across the room. Black Jack Brannigan stood in the shadowed doorway, drying his wet hair on a towel. Gone was the black gambler's hat with its silver conchos. Gone were the expensive linen shirt and the fancy embroidered satin vest. He wore a plain blue work shirt unbuttoned to the waist with the sleeves rolled up to his elbows. His black hair gleamed in the pale moonlight. Jack draped the towel around his neck and ran a hand through his damp hair.

"I'll thank you to keep your voice down, Mr. Brannigan," she hissed. She took Carrie back to bed and pulled the sheet over her legs. When she straightened, she saw Jack had followed her to the bedroom door.

He whispered. "Well, if you don't want me to disturb the little one, you might want to step into the kitchen with me."

Struck mute, she paused, trying to regain her attitude of distaste for the man. She squared her shoulders and crossed the room. The clean smell of soap teased her senses as she swept past him into the hallway.

Evangeline walked into the kitchen, scraped a match, and lit the lamp in the middle of the big oak table. Her hand trembled, a reaction that immensely annoyed her. Wasn't this the same rude man who'd insulted her yesterday, making her feel foolish and unattractive?

She looked up to see him standing at the kitchen door and scowled. "It certainly is considerate of you to finally show up here, Mr. Brannigan. I doubt it took you till well after dark to finish your work at the barn."

"Pardon me, Miss Gentry. The crossbeams on your barn roof were rotten. Tearing off the old shingles and cutting new beams took me a while longer than I'd anticipated. Finishing that, and putting on new boards and shingles will take me a day or two." He shrugged. "Sorry I couldn't whip that job off in a couple of hours for you."

He unfolded his arms and stood straighter. "But don't worry, I'll be here every afternoon to chop your wood when I'm done working on your barn."

He looked across the kitchen at the empty pots on the back of the stove. "I don't suppose there's a bite of supper left for me, is there?"

Shame flooded her at the realization he probably hadn't eaten since breakfast. "Of course," she answered. "I'll get you something right away."

He came to stand next to her while she took food from the warmer and filled a plate with leftover ham and potatoes. "I'm sorry I didn't get your supper out to you while it was hot." Her tone softened. "I was sidetracked with the children and laundry. Rachel and Mrs. Ingram and I were sewing their clothes and..."

Her voice trailed off when Jack took the plate and brushed her hand. He stood so close she could feel his warmth.

"No need to explain. I understand you had higher priorities than worrying about me. Why, I should probably be happy you agreed to feed me at all." He grinned, the curve of his lips lifting to reveal faint dimples.

Evangeline suddenly realized she'd been holding her breath. She backed up a step. "Please, sit down and eat. I'll get you a glass of milk. Or would you like me to reheat the coffee?"

"No, milk sounds good." Jack sat down at the table while she took a pitcher from the icebox and poured it into a glass. She could feel him looking her over in the same infuriating way he had at their previous run-ins.

"You know, you should wear your hair down like that all the time. It looks pretty that way."

"My hair is no concern of yours, Mr. Brannigan." She pulled her hair back and tucked the curly, wild strands into a loose bun. "Besides, I'm sure a man like you who spends his time in saloons is used to a fancier sort of woman than me."

"Oh, I don't know." He looked down at his plate. "I've seen some fancy women and some beautiful women in my time." He looked across the table at her. "But I've never seen anything to match the sight of you sitting in the moonlight a few minutes ago rocking a sick baby." He gave her a soft smile.

Evangeline felt herself blush and she self-consciously put a hand to her cheek. "Now, what a thing to say," was the only response she could muster. She walked to the screen door and stood looking out into the yard for a minute, then went out onto the porch. The breeze caressed her face, balmy and sweet with the scent of honeysuckle. She leaned against a column and closed her eyes, letting some of the day's tension drain from her.

Jack came up behind her, so close she could feel his nearness.

"Sorry if I embarrassed you." His voice was low and pleasant. "I have a habit of saying what I think, and that sometimes gets me into trouble."

His breath blew the hair on the back of her neck and sent a delicious sensation down her spine. Goosebumps formed on her arms and she ran her hands over them, but she didn't move away from him.

"Don't give it another thought, Mr. Brannigan. I'm just worn out and need to get a few hours' sleep. It's been a very long day." She turned and found herself looking up into his face.

"That it has. A long day for both of us. Why don't you go lie down for a couple of hours, and I'll listen for any little voices coming from the bedrooms. I'll sit out here on the porch until you wake up."

She wanted to say no but was too tired to pass up this offer of a nap. Besides, she couldn't think with him standing so close.

"Thank you, Mr. Brannigan, a short rest would be nice." Somehow, she couldn't resist the urge to throw a barb. "Then you can take a blanket out to the barn and get some sleep."

He flinched at the remark. Suddenly, the cynicism flooded back into his eyes and the tender tone in his voice turned sarcastic again. "Why, thank you, Evangeline, how very kind of you. And maybe tomorrow you'll let me borrow a pair of your pants to wear while I work on the roof for you."

She swayed in the wake of his rude comment. "I'll thank you not to call me by my given name. And yes, I do believe the reason you're here is to help take care of people less fortunate than yourself. Let's not forget the reason you landed in jail, to begin with, was because of your disorderly behavior." Her tone was crisp. "Now, you're stuck here doing manual labor, and you've had to trade in those fancy gambler's duds for work clothes."

Jack raised his eyebrows. "You're awfully judgmental, Miss High and Mighty. Maybe that's why you're still alone with only a cowpoke ranch foreman and his wife for company."

"I haven't married again by my own choice. I've had plenty of offers. As if that's any of your concern." She pushed past him and started for the door.

Jack gently touched her shoulder and turned her around to him. "I'm sorry, that remark was out of line."

She blinked back scalding tears. "I'm sure you meant it to be cruel, Mr. Brannigan. For some reason that's beyond me, you've insulted me at our every meeting." Her voice was tight with fury. Angry as she felt, she still noticed how his dark eyes turned down at the corners and how strong his hands felt.

Jack hung his head. "I'm sorry. I won't make that mistake again. I must have been crazy for thinking a woman like you wouldn't have men pounding her door down. Goodnight, Miss Gentry. You go on and get some rest. I'll sit right here on the porch. If either of those little ones wakes up while you're sleeping, I'll take care of whatever they need." Jack sat down in the rocker under the window and propped his feet on the porch rail. "And as tired as I am, I surely hope they don't need a thing."

Chapter Seven

Evangeline opened her eyes. A gray light filtered through the window. What was that smell? She turned onto her back, stretched, and sniffed the air again. Bacon. Why was breakfast cooking? At the clang of a dropped utensil in the kitchen, she started. Her hands covered her mouth. *Oh, no!* She'd slept through the night and failed to relieve Mr. Brannigan of his watch over the children.

She jumped out of bed and dashed to the chifforobe to get clean clothes. The arrogant face of Jack Brannigan popped into her mind again, and his derisive words about her work clothes rang in her ears. *Serves him right.* One night sleeping on a porch and checking in on sick children couldn't hurt the arrogant rat.

She picked up the dirty trousers and shirt from the floor of her chifforobe. *I should wear them just to spite him.* But she pulled a pale blue dress from its hanger instead. After a quick wash, Evangeline dressed and went into the kitchen where Rachel had breakfast almost ready to serve.

"Why didn't you wake me when you came in this morning?" She sped to the sink and tied on an apron. "I'll stir up some eggs for scrambling."

"Already done," Rachel said. "I figured you needed the extra sleep, and it was no trouble to start breakfast."

Evangeline looked around the kitchen for something that needed doing, but Rachel had everything under control. "I'll go look in on the children. I didn't hear a peep out of them last night. They must have rested well. I wonder if Jack Brannigan had to carry many drinks of water, or change any diapers."

She opened Noah's door and smiled at the sight of his tousled blond head on the pillow. "Noah, wake up. Breakfast is almost ready."

He opened his drowsy eyes and yawned. "Yes ma'am, I'm awake." Noah sat up and inhaled. "Something sure does smell good."

Evangeline slipped quietly into Carrie's room. This was what she'd always wanted, what was missing from her life. How many times had she passed the extra bedroom doors, and wished her own children were behind them? These little ones weren't hers, but she could pamper them for a while. She went to the bed and touched Carrie's forehead to see if her fever was down. Still warm, but better this morning.

She returned to the kitchen and poured herself some coffee. The back door burst open, and Rusty's long legs crossed the threshold. Behind him, Jack Brannigan came up the steps whistling a carefree tune, a pail of cold milk in his hand.

Her heart lurched at the sight of him with his broad shoulders and dark, wavy hair. She set her cup on the counter and smoothed the sides of her skirt.

Jack strolled into the kitchen and held the pail of milk out to her. She winced as his eyes raked her from her face to her toes and back up again. His whistle lowered and rose in pitch and volume in unison with his eyes.

Her cheeks burned with embarrassment. Why, why, why did that man look her over that way every time they met? She stiffened and took the pail from him.

Rusty turned to her. "Ain't he cheerful for somebody that slept on the porch all night?"

Jack grinned and nodded. "Good morning, Miss Gentry. Did you sleep well?"

She fiddled with the pockets of her apron and retied the bow in back. "I'm sorry I didn't wake up last night as I promised. I assure you, I had no intention of sleeping through the night."

She poured the milk into a pitcher and set it in the icebox. Wiping her hands on her apron, she turned back to him. "So you did sleep on the porch all night, Mr. Brannigan?" She picked up the coffee pot and started filling cups all around the table.

"That I did," he said. "All night. On the porch. In a hard chair." He put a hand to his lower back and rubbed it dramatically. "But I'm happy to report the children slept like logs. I checked on them a couple of times, and I don't mind telling you if I'd smelled a stinky diaper, I'd have pounded on your bedroom door." He eyed the pile of bacon and scrambled eggs on the table.

"Have a seat, Mr. Brannigan. Breakfast is ready." She poured hot gravy into a deep serving bowl.

"After the way you told me off last night, I wasn't sure I'd be welcome at your table." He scraped back a chair and sat down.

"Of course, you're welcome to eat with us. After all, you've got a long, hard day of work ahead of you, and you'll need your strength. There's the roof to finish, wood to chop, horses and cows to feed, fences to mend, and a lot of other chores that have gone undone while Rusty and I are off our usual schedules."

Jack almost choked on his coffee. "Don't you have any other hands here on this ranch, Miss Gentry? Do you expect me to take over the work of half a dozen people for the next month?"

"We're a small crew here, Mr. Brannigan. Rusty, Zeke, Charlie, and I take care of all the outdoor work. Rachel tends to most of the indoor duties, but I help with those, too, when I can." She leaned against the sideboard and crossed her arms. "There won't be much time to play cards, or drink around here."

Noah shuffled sleepily into the kitchen and took an empty chair next to Jack. He eyed him with curiosity.

Jack smiled and held out his hand. "You must be Noah. I'm Jack Brannigan. Some folks call me Black Jack."

Noah's eyes grew large. He looked at him, awestruck. "Are you a gunslinger, Black Jack?"

Jack laughed. "No, son, I'm not a gunslinger."

Evangeline thrust her hands to her hips and smirked. "No, he's a professional gambler, Noah. Some would say that's almost as bad."

Noah shifted his attention to Evangeline. "A gambler? You mean one of them men that rides on the riverboats and drinks and plays cards all night?"

She laughed. "You're exactly right, Noah. One of those men."

"Black Jack, what's it like to ride on those big

boats? Has anyone ever fell into those big paddle wheels? Have you ever got to drive one? You must be rich, huh?"

Jack laughed and held up a hand. "One question at a time, please!" He unfolded his napkin and draped it across his lap. "No, I'm not rich, but until I was robbed a couple of days ago, I did have enough money to pay my entry fee into the biggest poker tournament in San Francisco."

Noah hung on Jack's every word, his eyes huge with awe. "How much money did you lose, Black Jack?"

Jack frowned. "Over five thousand dollars."

Rusty hung his hat on the back of his chair and sat down. "Are we gonna eat breakfast before it's cold, or are we gonna jaw all mornin'?"

Noah looked up at Evangeline. "Ain't you gonna eat, ma'am?"

"Yes, of course, I am, Noah."

The chair on Jack's opposite side was empty. He looked up at her, his smile insolent.

She huffed and took a chair on the opposite side of the table next to Rachel. "Rusty, will you say grace?"

All heads bowed as Rusty asked the Lord's blessing on their food.

"Thank You, Lord, for the provision of this fine food we have here before us. Make us truly grateful...all of us...for what we're about to receive. And please, Lord, don't let anyone at this here table think they can slide by on a little bit of work and still enjoy Your gracious bounty. Amen."

"Miss Gentry," Jack began as the bowl of gravy came around the table. "I suppose you'll want me to get back to that roof right after breakfast?"

"Yes, of course, I do. The spring rains come sudden this time of year, and we can't afford to lose any of that hay."

Rusty looked up from his plate. "I reckon I'd best get out there and inspect what you've already done before you go any further," he said through a mouthful of food. "I wouldn't be happy about having to redo your work later."

"You sure you're up to it, Rusty?" Jack gave him an impudent smile.

"Don't you worry 'bout me, gambler."

Noah studied Jack between bites of crisp bacon. "Black Jack, can I come out and help you work on the barn after breakfast?"

"Well, I don't know." Jack glanced at Evangeline. "I wouldn't mind having a good helper like you, but that would be up to Miss Gentry."

Everyone turned to her, waiting for a response.

She looked around the table and laid her fork down next to her plate. "Noah, I'm not sure you're ready to work out in the sun yet. Let's give it a day or two, then we'll talk about it again." She sipped her coffee.

"And by the way, I don't think Black Jack is an appropriate name for you to use. I think you should call him Mr. Brannigan."

"Yes, ma'am, Miss Gentry."

She lowered her cup again. "But you can call me Evangeline."

"Oh, no, ma'am, I couldn't do that. My ma would have skinned me alive for calling you by your given name."

Rusty offered a solution. "Why don't you call her Miss Eva like me and the ranch hands do?"

Noah grinned. "Miss Eva? Yes, ma'am, that's better. I'll call you that."

~

Jack looked up at the sound of Carrie moving around and fussing.

Evangeline wiped her mouth and pushed back from the table.

"Sounds like somebody's tuning up in there," Rusty looked toward the door and reached for another biscuit.

Evangeline grabbed a tray she'd prepared earlier and hurried across the sun-dappled kitchen floor.

"Let me help you with that." Jack hopped up from the table and followed her to Carrie's room. Her dress showed off her small waistline to perfection. What a difference from the baggy pants and shirt. He brushed her arm as he reached around her and opened the bedroom door.

Evangeline set the tray down on the dresser and raised the window shade. Bright morning sun filtered through the lacy curtain, mottling the pale-yellow counterpane with sunlight.

She put a small dose of quinine in a cup of water. "Mr. Brannigan, would you grab a diaper from that top drawer?"

Jack handed her the diaper and looked around the room, noting the bed, side table, dresser, and the rocker by the window. "There isn't much room left in here, but that little girl needs a crib." He sat on the edge of the bed while Evangeline pinned a clean diaper on Carrie. "She'll climb out of this bed and run around the house while you sleep after a few days of rest and good food."

Evangeline raised an eyebrow at him. "Do you have children, Mr. Brannigan? You seem to know so much about them."

"No. I've never been married. But I helped with my little brother, Jesse, and I seem to recall that they need a lot of corralling at this age."

Evangeline moved to the rocker with Carrie. Her golden-brown hair was haloed in the morning sun.

Jack remembered how she'd been every bit as beautiful sitting in the parlor last night, with the moonlight beaming in on her. "Well, I'd better get to work on that barn now. I know you're in a hurry for me to finish so I can get back here and chop wood." He winked at her and disappeared out the door.

Evangeline shook her head as he walked out the door. "What a confusing man you are, Mr. Brannigan."

~

Jack paused at the back door. "I'm heading out to the meadow now, Cunningham." He pushed his hat on. "You coming along to inspect?"

Rusty put his empty coffee cup in the dishpan and sauntered over to Jack. Rusty, who stood just as tall and broad-shouldered but lanky and raw-boned, met Jack's defiant gaze.

"Yeah, I'm ready, Brannigan."

"You sure you can get back on that roof with one arm in a sling? Maybe you should get one of the other hands to climb up and inspect it for you."

"There ain't no other hands right now, as you well know."

Noah jumped to his feet. "I'll 'spect it for you. I can climb real good." Something about Noah reminded Jack of his brother Jesse. Maybe it was his spunk and the way he liked to tag along.

Jack laughed and patted the boy on the head. "I wouldn't mind, Noah, but you heard what Miss Gentry said. Maybe in a day or two."

Noah frowned. "Aw, I suppose I'll have to spend the day toting water for Miss Eva and feeding horses again."

"There's no shame in toting water or feeding horses. I sure did my share of both when I was your age. Maybe later you can lend me a hand on the roof. Or better yet, maybe I'll teach you a few things about horses. Can you ride bareback?"

Noah perked up. "No sir. You can show me how to do that?"

"You bet. I can and I will. Now, you go on and do what Miss Gentry and Rachel tell you to do today. And I think it's okay if you call me Jack from now on."

Noah beamed up at him. "Yes, sir, Jack. I sure will." He raced out the door to start his chores, Chester close on his heels.

Jack turned back to Rusty. A frown creased his brow. "You know, that boy just lost his mother. It might be a good thing to let him spend time with me doing something physical, instead of staying indoors all day."

THE GAMBLE ON LOVE

Rusty nodded his head. "I reckon you might be right about that. I'll talk to Miss Eva and see if she'll let him come out to the barn for an hour or two later this afternoon. You get on out to the hay barn, and I'll be there directly. I need to have a word with Rachel."

Jack strode out the door and crossed the backyard, past the pink peonies blooming in the sun and the hedge of wild roses. He vaulted the fence into the east pasture where Evangeline's colts frolicked with their mothers. Some nibbled on the spring grass and some lazed under the low branches of apple trees loaded with blossoms. He strolled past the big horse barn and dipped into the glen where the hay barn awaited his attention.

Jack gathered the tools he'd need today and then made his way to the back of the barn to get wood shingles. Behind the shingles, he spotted a stack of fine pale oak and dropped the tools he held. He picked up one of the oak planks and ran his hand along the grain, admiring its texture and beauty.

"Now a man could make a fine piece of furniture out of this." Boyhood memories of working alongside his father in his cooper's shop ran through his mind. The workbench lined with adze, drawknives, and planes. The fragrant aroma of the wood curls collected in piles around his father's feet. Memories of life before his father died—before his mother remarried a man who got drunk and beat her.

Jack laid the oak board back onto the stack, returned outside, and climbed the ladder with a stack of shingles. He got busy hammering, but his mind was busy planning what he wanted to make with that oak in the barn.

65

Chapter Eight

Rusty and Reverend Ingram flopped into chairs on the front porch. The reverend fanned himself with his hat.

Rusty adjusted his sling and rubbed his shoulder. "Thanks for helping me get the hay out to them cattle, Reverend. For a man of the cloth, you'd make a right good ranch hand."

"Well, I've fed my flock at church for many years," Reverend Ingram mopped the back of his neck with a handkerchief. "But this kind of feeding certainly works up a bigger sweat."

Rusty's stomach growled as the aroma of frying chicken drifted through the window. "Must be about dinnertime."

The front door opened and Evangeline stepped onto the porch with tall glasses of lemonade. "I thought you two could use something cold to drink." She handed the men their drinks and sat on the porch rail. "Dinner will be ready in a few minutes." She watched them gulp down their lemonade.

Evangeline studied one of several ferns swinging in the breeze at the corner of the porch and hooked her feet around the spindles. "Tell Rachel not to worry about the dishes. I'll do them after I take Mr. Brannigan his meal." She kept her eyes on the swaying fern, so as to avoid eye contact with Rusty. "Then after you eat, I'd like you to make a trip into town and withdraw the breeding stock money and take it straight to Mr. Wainwright. I don't want to risk missing him before he leaves for Kansas City."

"Will do, Miss Eva." He propped his huge feet up on the rail and tipped back on the hind legs of his chair. "By the way," he began, his drawl slower than usual, "you reckon it's a good idea for you to be taking food out to Brannigan? He's a mighty untrustworthy sort of feller, you know." He peered up at her from under the brim of his hat. "A no-account gambler, I think you called him."

She untangled her legs from the porch rail. Her eyes widened as she peered at Rusty. "Yes, I did say that. But the man *is* working out there in the heat to repair my barn, so I think he deserves a good meal for his efforts."

"I'd be more than happy to take it out to him, Evangeline," Reverend Ingram offered with absolutely no guile.

"Thank you, Reverend, but I'll do it." She fumbled with the hem of her apron. "I feel quite guilty for not getting his dinner out to him yesterday. And I need a walk anyway, so I'll take it to him."

Rusty harumphed and pulled his hat low over his eyes. "Just watch out for that man. I don't trust him."

~

Evangeline took the long way down to the meadow where the faded red barn stood under the sturdy branches of an oak tree. The trail from the main road wound through a tangle of wild sumac and over a brook where she stopped in the lush, green dell. In the distance, Jack bent over his work on the roof.

She tucked in a loose strand of hair, straightened her collar, and approached the barn. "Mr. Brannigan, I've brought you your dinner."

A dark head peeked over the edge of the roof. Jack turned around and started down the ladder making quick work of the rungs. His shirt was damp with sweat, and she could see the play of the muscles in his back as he made his way down to the ground.

"It wasn't my imagination, then," he said. "I thought I smelled fried chicken and strawberry pie on the breeze." He pulled back the napkin that covered the basket. "What do you have in here?"

"Fried chicken and strawberry pie," she laughed. "Along with a few other things."

They made their way to the shade of the oak. Evangeline spread a cloth on the ground and laid out crispy chicken with all the trimmings and the strawberry pie Jack had smelled in the air.

He hurried to the brook where he washed up, then he returned and sat beside her. The smile on his tan face was the first genuine smile she had seen cross his lips since they'd met. He seemed so pleased at the small gesture of bringing him a meal.

"It all looks delicious." His eyes were dark as obsidian and gleaming with life. They turned down at the corners, giving him a perpetual drowsy look. "And it seems you'll honor me by eating with me?"

"Everything would be cold by the time I walked back home so I might as well eat with you."

Jack rubbed his hands together. "This looks like a special Sunday dinner to me."

She filled a plate with green beans and German potato salad and handed him the bowl of chicken so he could choose his favorite piece. When Jack reached out, his bicep filled the sleeve of his blue work shirt, as snug as a hand in a glove. His rolled-up sleeves revealed thick, finely corded forearms. *How does a gambler build up muscles like those?*

Evangeline leaned back against the tree trunk and took a dainty bite of her chicken. "How is the roof coming along, Mr. Brannigan?"

"Faster than I'd expected. I may even finish by tomorrow afternoon. The next day for sure." She noticed the damp curls at the nape of his neck, then moved her gaze back to his face.

"So soon?" She took another nibble. "That will leave a lot of time to fill while you work off your thirty days," she said. "Well, with Rusty on light duty, I'm sure he'll be able to keep you busy."

Jack frowned. "Rusty. Now there's a man who doesn't want me around this ranch at all. He seems to think he needs to protect you from me."

"Oh, Rusty's more than my foreman. He's been my friend since my late husband and I moved here from Kentucky. He and Rachel think it's their job to look out for me. I wouldn't let it bother me too much if I were you."

He nodded his understanding.

"Mr. Brannigan, I meant to tell you, Rachel and Rusty said you're welcome to stay in their cabin. No need for you to sleep in the barn when they have a comfortable bed you can use."

"I'm fine in the barn. I'd feel like an intruder staying in their home, but thank them anyway. In fact, with the weather so nice, I was thinking I might make my bed out here under the trees."

Evangeline shook her head and raised an eyebrow at him. "I can't figure you out, Mr. Brannigan. You're a gambler, there's no question about that, but you can roof a barn without assistance, and you want to sleep outdoors." She wagged a chicken leg at him. "You have the look of a man who has done hard work. I mean you're no scrawny little indoor type."

Jack tossed his head back and laughed, the sound a sonorous baritone. "Why thank you, ma'am."

She felt her face flush. "Oh, you know what I mean. You can tell when a man is all pale and puny that he's never put in a good day's work in his life." She peered up at him. Was she was saying too much? "You look like you've done your share of hard work."

Jack set his plate down and braced a tanned forearm around one upraised knee. "Miss Gentry, as I told the Reverend a couple of days ago, I wasn't born to the gambling life. I had a father who taught me how to do a man's work and a mother who taught me the difference between right and wrong." He laughed. "She made my brother Jesse and me memorize Bible verses. I even won a Bible in Sunday School for it."

He pulled a blade of grass and twirled it between his fingers. "I've taken some detours along the road, but when the time comes – when I meet the right lady, I'll know how to take care of a family."

Evangeline found herself staring at Jack, lost in the image of him mending fences, green breaking colts, and reciting Bible verses in Sunday School. She swallowed her bite of chicken and gazed out over the meadow. "Yes, you are a contradiction, Mr. Brannigan."

He took a sip of lemonade. "I don't suppose there's any chance I could persuade you to call me Jack, is there?"

"Well, I agree Mr. Brannigan sounds a bit formal, but Jack seems too familiar." She laughed and shrugged.

"Okay, maybe you'd settle for calling me John Aaron, which would still be better than Mr. Brannigan."

"John Aaron." She arched an eyebrow. "That's your given name?" She looked away for a moment. "Very nice name. I like it. But I suppose I'll call you Jack. It does seem to suit you."

He nodded at her. "By golly, I think you're right. It does suit me. A Jack of all trades and master of none." He reached for another piece of chicken. "By the way, your name certainly suits you. Evangeline...a beautiful and graceful name for a beautiful, graceful woman."

Evangeline giggled and gave a small shrug. No sooner had she opened her mouth to speak than the sound of feet splashing through the brook and a dog's bark caused her to look up. Noah raced down the hill toward them, Chester trotting behind. "Noah, what are you doing here? Have you finished your dinner already?"

"Yes, ma'am. It don't take me long to eat." He flung himself to the ground. "Ain't she a good cook, Jack?" he asked. "That's better potato salad than my grandma used to make."

"You bet she's a good cook. This is a meal fit for royalty." Jack took another bite and rubbed his stomach with satisfaction.

"Oh, stop it now, both of you." Evangeline packed the bowl of chicken back into her basket and fussed with the napkins.

"I'm gonna help you now, Jack," Noah beamed. "Rusty and Miss Eva told me I could help after dinner."

"With a fine helper like you, I'll be done in no time." Jack finished his meal.

She packed up her basket and walked toward the footpath.

"Evangeline, wait! I found a stack of oak lumber in the barn. Is it meant for any special purpose?"

"No, it's leftover from the floors in the house. Why?"

"I was just wondering. So, it's okay if I use it?"

"Sure, if you need it, you're welcome to it."

Jack gave her a sly smile. "I might be able to put it to good use."

She turned to Noah. "And you help Mr. Brannigan with his work. Be home in time for supper." She looked at Jack. "Both of you."

~

Jack grabbed Noah's arm as the boy started up the ladder, the loose sole of his boot catching on a rung.

"Wait, Noah. Come into the barn, I've got another project I want to work on." He led Noah to the back of the barn and dragged out the stack of oak he'd seen earlier.

"What's that for?"

"This is fine oak wood. Good for making furniture, and we're going to make a bed for Carrie. But don't tell Miss Eva. It'll be a surprise."

"Oh, she'll like that, all right. Ladies always love surprises." He glanced up at him. "You know how to make furniture?"

Jack nodded. "My father taught me to craft furniture, raise a house or a barn, and build the finest barrels and casks in the state of Connecticut, or probably anywhere else for that matter." He caressed the wood like it was a living thing. "My father was a cooper." He held his head up and said it with pride. "And he taught me to work with wood, too." He looked at Noah, who stared up at him, wide-eyed. "And I can teach you some things, too, if you want to learn."

"I sure do, Jack." He picked up one of the boards and stroked it, mimicking his behavior.

"We'll have to get some special tools together, so we need to go into town." *And I can pay a visit to that crooked barkeep at the Golden Eagle Saloon.* He laid his hat on a bale of hay and slid the lumber back onto the stack.

Noah picked up the hat and traced the delicate engraving on the sterling silver conchos. "Boy, these sure are some fancy things on your hat." The boy's face lit up. "I'll bet this must have cost you a million dollars."

Jack chuckled. "No, not quite that much, but they are valuable." He came and sat down on the bale of hay. "You're one of the few men I've ever allowed to handle my lucky conchos."

Noah grinned in response. "Lucky conchos? What's so lucky about 'em?"

Jack scratched his stubbly jaw. "Well, it's a long story, but right after I got home from the fighting in Connecticut, I was–well, restless. I was a young fellow of eighteen years when the war finished, and I didn't know what to do with myself. My mother and father were both gone, like yours are, Noah." He put a hand on the child's thin shoulder.

"I ended up going into a saloon and playing cards with a man who was dressed more elegantly than I'd ever seen anyone dressed. He wore a fine suit of black broadcloth and a vest made of satin with silver threads embroidered into it. He was wearing a hat with this band of conchos on it." He pointed to the hat Noah held as if it were a crown filled with rare jewels.

"That man invited me to sit and play cards at his table. I had what you call 'beginners' luck' that night and was winning big. But that wasn't the lucky part." He smiled as he continued telling Noah the story. "The lucky part was when the man took this band of silver conchos off his hat and threw it into the middle of the table along with all the money he had."

Jack gazed up at the rafters and grimaced as he remembered. "You see, Noah, he was going to deal from the bottom of the deck, and he knew he would win all the money everyone had when he dealt the next few cards."

"Well, as young and green as I was, and as fast as he was with his hands, I saw him take his cards from the bottom of the deck and I told him so. There was a fight and some shooting, but I ended up leaving the saloon with this hatband and a big pile of money. Ever since that day, I've had good luck at playing cards.

That's why I've always considered it my lucky hatband."

Noah's eyes opened as big as saucers. "Wow, Jack. Can you teach me how to play cards like that?"

"No." He shook his head and turned to look Noah in the eye. "No, I won't teach you to play cards." Jack fixed Noah with a stern expression. "Even though I've made a lot of money gambling, it's a bad way to spend your life. I've spent many nights sitting in a smoke-filled room with drunken men who were spending money they should have used to feed their families." He shook his head again. "No, it's a bad life, Noah, and not for a boy like you."

He walked to the barn door and stared out across the meadow. "Nope. You need to learn the things somebody like Miss Gentry can teach you. Go to church and learn how to be a good man."

Noah laid the hat down on the lid of a barrel and said quietly, "But, Jack. How come you're going to that fancy poker game in California if gambling is a bad thing to do?"

Jack felt like he'd been sucker-punched. His shoulders bunched in reaction, but he didn't turn around. "I've been doing it so long it's about all I know how to do." The words sounded hollow and phony even to *his* ears.

"But you said you know how to make furniture and barrels like your father did. Why don't you do that instead of gambling?"

Jack needed to change the subject. He pasted a smile on his face and spun around to Noah. "I am good at making furniture and, starting tomorrow, I'm going to teach you how to use a plane to smooth these oak boards."

He looked at the pile of boards against the wall. "It won't be fancy. I don't have a lathe or the other tools I need to make it the way I'd like to, but I saw a pretty good draw knife for sale at the mercantile. We can still make a handsome and sturdy piece of furniture. Let's get back to work on this roof and tomorrow after lunch, we'll go into town and get some tools."

Chapter Nine

Evangeline crossed the backyard humming and swinging her wicker basket. The screen door squeaked open and Rusty stepped out onto the porch wearing a look of disapproval that made her feel like a guilty schoolgirl.

"Well, it appears like you had a nice picnic, Miss Eva."

"It wasn't a picnic, Rusty, it was just a plain old dinner."

"Plain old dinner, huh? The last time you made German potato salad was for the Founder's Day celebration, and we usually only get pie for Sunday dinner."

Evangeline climbed the steps onto the back porch. "Rusty, please stop exaggerating." She edged past him and put the basket on the sideboard. "Are you ready to go into town for me? Remind Mr. Dibble at the bank that you have a signature card on file so you can sign a bank draft on my account."

"I suppose I'm ready. Would you write a little note to Mr. Dibble and..."

The sound of Doc O'Brien's raucous laughter came from the bedroom.

"Oh, Doc is here? You didn't tell me that." She threw her shawl over the back of the kitchen chair and hurried into the bedroom. Doc sat in a chair beside the bed taking a sarsaparilla stick from his medical bag.

"It sounds like someone is having a lot of fun in this sick room." She laughed.

"Afternoon, Evangeline! This little gal is much better today, I can see that." He handed her the candy and tucked the sheet around Carrie's waist. "Her temperature is almost normal, and Noah is looking strong. In fact, I think it's safe to say he won't contract the grippe."

"I'm glad to hear you think they're doing so well." She idly stroked Carrie's hair. "Although, of course, I knew they were. Their appetite is good, and Carrie's color was better this morning."

"Yes, her color is definitely better." Doc closed his bag and leaned back in the rocker. "You know, I think Carrie had already suffered the worst of it before you found her." He lowered his voice. "Both children are mighty lucky they made it this far. And mighty lucky you got to them when you did."

He put his hands on the chair arms and pushed himself up. "Well, whatever you're doing, keep it up. I'll get back out here sometime tomorrow afternoon and check on them again. I'd say if Carrie keeps improving at this rate, I'll lift the quarantine by Friday or Saturday. You can probably take them to church with you on Sunday."

She grinned from ear to ear. "Really, Doc? That's wonderful! Did you hear that, Carrie?" She turned to the little girl. "You're getting better!"

Doc pinched Carrie's cheek. "This one needs a crib because she'll be up and about any day now."

"Yes, someone else mentioned that earlier."

Evangeline picked Carrie up and wiped sticky candy from her chin. "Sunday morning I'll put you in your pink dress with hair ribbons, and I'll have Noah spit-shined and polished. I can't wait to show you both off to the whole town."

Doc put an arm around Evangeline and they walked together into the kitchen. He gave her a solemn look. "Dear, I know it's not my place to say this, but I will anyway. Be careful not to get so attached to these young'uns that it breaks your heart when you have to separate from them."

Her smile faded. "I know you're right, Doc. I've been thinking about talking to a lawyer about adoption. If they don't have any other relatives, and if Noah is willing, I'd like to raise them as my own."

Doc raised a bushy eyebrow. "Is that so? Well, if you're sure, talk to Albert Mitchell. He's a friend of mine and a good lawyer." He stopped at the back door. "Give it a lot of thought and prayer before you make any big moves, Evangeline."

"I will, Doc," she promised. She kissed the old man on the cheek.

"Rusty, you take care of things around this place," he said over his shoulder.

Rusty rolled his eyes. "Oh, I'm trying, Doc. I'm trying."

~

A knock sounded at the kitchen door as Evangeline turned down the lamp on the dining table.

She opened the door, expecting to see Rusty or Rachel standing there. "Jack!" A wave of surprise washed through her.

"Evening, Miss Gentry. I've finished working on the barn and wanted to let you know that I'm getting ready to start splitting some wood for you." Thunder rumbled in the distance and a gust of air ruffled the curtains beside the door. Jack looked tired—his shoulders sagged and he leaned against the doorframe.

"There's no need to start that this evening. It's already getting late, and I think it will be raining soon. Wood can wait until morning. You've already chopped enough to last a month, anyway. Why don't you come on in and have a glass of iced tea before you head out to the barn for the night?"

Jack opened his mouth to answer when they were interrupted by an excited young voice. "Is that you, Jack?" They heard a thud, followed by the sound of two feet racing down the hallway toward the kitchen. "Jack, what are you doing here? Are you going to come in for a while?"

Evangeline crossed her arms over her chest and made her best attempt to sound firm. "Young man, you were supposed to be getting ready for bed. I'll be in soon to hear your prayers."

"But Miss Eva, can't I have some iced tea with you and Jack and then he can listen to my prayers, too?"

Evangeline started to explain that Jack was tired

from a long day, but he smiled broadly at Noah. "Noah, I think it's your bedtime, but I'd be honored to hear your prayers. I promise we can have that iced tea together tomorrow evening."

Noah scampered back down the hallway and then kneeled at the side of his bed. Evangeline got on her knees beside him while Jack propped himself against the wall.

Noah bowed his head and whispered his prayer. "Thank You, God, that Carrie ain't sick anymore. And thank You that Miss Eva takes such good care of us. And please, God, say hello to Ma and Pa and Gramps for me."

Evangeline quickly swiped tears from her eyes as Noah crawled into bed. She tucked him in and planted a kiss on his forehead.

Noah looked at Jack expectantly. "My gramps used to tell me a story at night."

She suspected Noah was trying to keep Jack there for as long as possible, but he smiled and pulled a rocking chair near the bed. "Well now. Let me see if I can remember any good stories."

Noah smiled with apparent satisfaction and adjusted his pillow.

Jack scratched his square jaw and looked from Noah to Evangeline. "Once upon a time, there was a boy named Jack that lived with his poor old widowed mother. One day his mother came to him and said, 'Jack, our cupboards are empty and we have nothing left to eat. You must take our cow to the market and sell it so we can buy some food.'"

She smiled, knowing this fairytale of Jack and the Beanstalk from her childhood.

Lightning flashed much closer this time, followed quickly by a loud roll of thunder. Jack leaned forward and continued. "Early the next morning, Jack and the cow set off for the market but, about halfway to town, Jack saw a man sitting at the side of the road. 'Little boy, come over here. Where are you going with that fine-looking cow?' he asked. "'I'm going to town to sell it so my mother can buy some food,' came his reply.

"'Well, why don't you sit here with me, and we'll cut this deck of cards. If I get the highest card, I'll get the cow, but if you get the highest card, I'll give you these five magic beans.'"

"Jack Brannigan!" Evangeline shouted. "That's not the way that story goes!"

"Well, that's the way *I* remember it," Jack said, a sheepish grin on his face.

Noah rolled back and forth, laughing riotously. "I like it, Jack! Finish the story."

"Never mind," Evangeline said. "You get to sleep, young man. Maybe Jack can refresh his memory on how this fairytale goes and try again another night."

Jack got up from his chair and went to Noah, sitting beside him on the bed. He tousled the boy's hair and squeezed his shoulder. "Miss Eva's right. I'd better get that story straight before I go on with it." He blew out the light, and he and Evangeline left the room, leaving the door slightly ajar. "I don't suppose I could still get that glass of iced tea, could I?"

"Certainly." She relit the lamp on the table. Lightning streaked the sky, followed by a nerve-shattering boom that rattled the windows.

"That one sounded like it hit something." Jack's

eyes moved to the window.

"Yes, it sure did. I hope this storm doesn't wake Carrie." She went to the window and pulled back the curtain, scanning the yard. "If I know Rusty, he'll be out there checking on things right away. He'll let us know if there's a problem."

She filled their glasses and handed him one. "You know, despite the way you butchered that fairytale, you made Noah very happy tonight. I don't think I've ever heard him laugh like that." She handed him the glass.

"Well, that's what I was hoping for."

"Of course, I should have realized that." She took a partially eaten pie from the icebox, cut slices for them, and sat down across from Jack.

"Thank you, Miss Gentry." Jack downed half the contents of his glass in one long swallow. He yawned and rubbed his hands over his eyes. "I guess I'm a little more tired than I realized. But the barn roof is almost finished. I should be done tomorrow and I don't think this rain tonight will cause any problems."

"You know, Jack, I understand the circumstances that brought you here to help, and I'm sure you'd rather be just about anywhere else, but I truly do appreciate all the work you've done here on my ranch. You've been a tremendous help."

He smiled the warm smile that made her heart flutter – the one that deepened his dimples and made his dark eyes sparkle. "Well, thank you for saying that. And since we're on the subject, I'd like to make a long-overdue, sincere apology for the way I spoke to you the day we met in town. I was extremely rude and my only excuse is that I'd had way too much to drink at the saloon."

She took a sip of her iced tea. "Thank you, Jack, although I know I must have looked horrible when you saw me."

He reached across the table and lightly touched her hand. "No, don't say that. Even in my drunken state, I thought you were one of the loveliest sights I'd ever seen."

She blushed and pushed a stray curl behind her ear. "Thank you"

"No, don't thank me. I mean every word of it. Frankly, I can't imagine how you handle this place alone. I mean, I know you have Rusty and a couple of ranch hands, but you've kept this place up beautifully. Not many young women could do what you do."

"Well, I've been running this place alone for over three years now, since my husband died. It's hard sometimes, but Rusty and Rachel make things so much easier for me. I'd be lost without them." The sound of raindrops hitting the roof brought Evangeline back to the here and now. "It sounds like the rain is about to let loose."

"Yes, I'd better get out to the barn, or I'll end up getting drenched." He scooped up the last bite of his pie and shoved his hat on.

"Thank you for the tea and the nice conversation," he said as he reached the door. "And tell Noah I'll try and remember the way that bedtime story really goes."

She laughed and turned the doorknob. "I'll do that. You can be sure he'll expect you to finish the story for him." Evangeline pushed open the screen door.

Jack stepped out into the night. "Just sprinkling out here." He turned up his collar.

"Good night, Jack. I'll see you bright and early for

breakfast."

Jack started down the steps and Evangeline closed the screen door.

"Fire!" Rusty ran into the yard at a ground-eating pace. "Lightening hit the big horse barn. It's on fire!"

Rachel flew up the steps, out of breath. "Evangeline, do you have a couple of old quilts? We will need something to beat the fire with."

Evangeline ran to her bedroom just off the kitchen. She grabbed a stack of blankets off the top of her chifforobe and sprinted back towards the door. "Rachel, stay with the children. I'm going out to the barn."

Rachel grabbed Evangeline's wrist before she could open the back door. "No, please–you stay here."

"I'm going, Rachel. This ranch is my responsibility. I won't let you risk your life while I sit here doing nothing."

Rachel started to protest, but Evangeline wasn't listening. She was already out the door with Jack two steps ahead of her.

They raced across the yard and toward the meadow. Evangeline could already see smoke and a few fingers of fire above the tree line. Rusty was inside releasing horses from their stalls when they reached the barn.

Jack grabbed one of the quilts and dipped it into the nearby trough, ran into the barn, and raced up the ladder into the loft. Evangeline ran in behind him, the smoke so thick she could barely see where Rusty stood. The horses were neighing wildly, terrified of the smoke, heat, and the crackling sound of burning roof timbers.

She pulled up her dress tail and covered her nose and mouth, feeling her way to the first stall. She could hear her favorite horse Scarlett's fearful snorting inside.

She raised the latch on the gate and opened it. Before she could get inside to rush Scarlett out the door, the mare reared up in fear, knocking Evangeline back into the wall, hitting her head hard against the corner post. She crumpled to the floor as Scarlett raced out the door, along with the horses Rusty released at the back of the barn.

~

Jack called down from the smoldering hay loft. "Cunningham!"

"Yeah, Brannigan?" Rusty coughed violently as he made his way to the next stall.

"I'm giving up on the loft," Jack shouted. "The hay is making this place a tinderbox. We need to concentrate on getting these horses out and saving ourselves. The fire is spreading too fast."

"Yes, let's get the last of these stalls opened and get out of here," Rusty agreed.

Jack took the first few rungs of the ladder and leaped the rest of the way down. Feeling his way through the thickening smoke, he opened the stall nearest him and took a step. Suddenly he felt his ankle touch something soft—something that felt a lot like human flesh.

"Evangeline?" He could barely see her, but there she lay at his feet. He scooped her up into his arms. "Cunningham! Miss Gentry has fainted. I'm getting her out of here!" He made his way out into the cool, fresh air, coughing violently. He laid her gently under a nearby tree and began to tap her cheeks to bring her around. "Evangeline, come on … wake up."

The last of the horses raced out of the barn and made their way into the meadow as Rusty wearily stumbled out into the fresh air. He knelt beside Evangeline as her eyes flickered open. "Miss Eva, you okay?"

"She's coming around. She'll be all right." Jack brushed stray locks of curly brown hair back from her face. "She's going to be okay."

The rain poured in earnest now. Rusty shouted over his shoulder. "Let me mount Copper and see if I can get these horses corralled. I'll meet you back at the house as soon as I can."

Jack nodded his approval. "Miss Gentry, can you sit up?"

Evangeline tried to raise herself into an upright position, then groaned. She put her hand to the back of her head and rubbed it gingerly.

"Are you okay? What's happened to your head?"

"I guess I hit it when I opened Scarlett's stall. I should have been more careful." She seemed to suddenly realize that she rested in Jack's arms and tried again to sit up, but he held her in place.

"Take it slowly, Evangeline. We don't know how badly you're hurt yet."

"I think I'm okay. I need to go help Rusty with the horses."

Jack chuckled. "You aren't going anywhere right now. Rusty's getting the horses corralled, and Rachel's with the children. You take a few minutes to make sure you're not hurt." He pushed back another wisp of her hair and allowed his fingers to slide down her cheek and brush her chin.

Evangeline swallowed hard and tried to push herself

up again. "The children."

"I told you, Rachel's with the children."

The rain shifted directions and pelted Jack's back. He picked her up again. "Let's get back to the house before you catch your death of cold."

"I can walk." She feebly struggled against him, but he held her as if she were a kitten.

"You hold still. I'm carrying you to the house, and that's the end of it."

~

Jack laid Evangeline down on the sofa in the living room and covered her with a soft blue afghan. "Promise me you'll rest here while Rusty and I check on the horses."

She started to protest, but Jack put a finger across her lips. "Promise."

Rachel carefully closed Carrie's bedroom door and paced over to Evangeline, her brow creased with worry. "Is Rusty okay?"

Jack nodded. "Yes, I'm on my way to help him round up the horses."

Rachel visibly relaxed. "The children have managed to sleep through all of this."

"See?" Jack squeezed Evangeline's hand. "Everything is fine. Maybe Rachel would make you a cup of tea?"

He met Rachel's eyes. "She probably shouldn't go to sleep for a while after that bump on the head, anyway. Rachel, I know it's late, but would you mind making sure Miss Gentry stays awake? At least until Rusty and I get through dealing with the horses?"

"Of course, Mr. Brannigan."

He tucked the afghan around Evangeline as if she were a child. "Good night, Miss Gentry. I'll see you in the morning."

~

Evangeline scooted higher on the couch and adjusted the pillow behind her back. She looked up as Rachel walked in with a tray holding a pot of tea and two cups. She sat it on the nearby table.

Rachel leaned over the tray, taking each delicate cup in hand and filling it with tea, the aroma permeating the room. She put a spoonful of sugar into each, then sunk into the rocking chair by Evangeline's side. She let out a heavy sigh and leaned her head against the back of the chair.

Evangeline took a sip of the hot brew. She looked over at her friend, her brow furrowed. "Are you okay, Rachel? You seem distraught."

Rachel sighed again and picked up her own tea. "You are right." She blew away the steam. "Ever since Rusty fell from the barn, I cannot seem to shake these images from my mind, of Rusty getting hurt, of me losing him." She gazed into the cup. "I see Rusty lying in the barn, severely injured by this fire." She gazed into the distance. "I worry I'll lose Rusty, who is everything to me. I worry I'll never hold a child of my own."

Evangeline straightened up and sat her tea on the table. She picked up the Bible she kept in her living room. "I understand. I had similar attacks of fear and anxiety after Jared died." A small smile tugged at her mouth. "What got me through was remembering what the Bible says: 'Casting all your care upon him; for he careth for you.' I had to learn to hand my troubles to Him. To pray, and let it go."

Rachel smiled in return and sat down her tea. "Thank you, Evangeline, for that reminder. That is just what I will do."

Evangeline chuckled. "Many a night I had to pick up my Bible and revisit that scripture." She ran a thumb over the pages of the book in her hands. "My Bible is chock full of little markers for verses from that bleak chapter in my life."

"Yes, I remember that terrible time, as well. Rusty suffered, too, when he lost his dear friend." A wistful look crossed her face. "Jared was a good man." Rachel stood, walked over, and wrapped her in a gentle hug.

Evangeline patted her back and smiled. "Your husband will be fine."

The door burst open and Rusty strode into the room, drenched but apparently unscathed. He snatched the hat from his head and slapped it against his leg, water droplets flying across the room. "Tarnation! Brannigan just got one roof put on and now we lose another one!" He sighed. "Good news is, though, that the rain started just in time. I think the barn's saved. He'll just need to put on another roof."

A soft smile spread across Rachel's face as Rusty turned to her.

"C'mon, Rachel, let's get up to our cabin."

"Okay, *Querida*. Let me get these dishes in the sink."

Evangeline shook her head. "Don't worry about the dishes. They'll be fine until morning. You two get home and get some rest." She watched as Rusty wrapped an arm around Rachel, walking by her side as they headed home. She looked around her empty living room. Her heart ached.

Chapter Ten

The sun rose bright and warm the morning after the storm. Jack and Noah rode into Independence and tied their horses in front of the mercantile. Jack clomped across the wooden sidewalk, his expensive snakeskin boots shining in the sunlight, and took a seat on the bench in front of the store. Noah followed close behind, his boot making a flip-flop sound as he walked.

"Ain't we goin' in, Jack?" he asked. "I thought you wanted to buy some things so we can build Carrie's crib."

Jack rubbed his chin and leaned down, his elbows resting on his knees. "Yes, we're going in. Just give me a minute. No rush." His eyes veered over to Noah's boots and then back to his own. The thought of the thousands of dollars he'd had only a few days ago burned in his mind. He looked at the boy, skinny and ragged, and wished he could do something about it.

Jack took his hat off and polished the conchos with his shirtsleeve. He sighed, went to his saddle, and pulled his gun from the saddlebag.

Noah's eyes went wide. "Why are you getting your gun out, Jack? You gonna shoot somebody?"

Jack laughed and tucked the gun into the front of his

pants. "If you aren't the most curious boy I've ever known. No, I'm not going to shoot anybody, but I need to do me a bit of bartering. You wait here, and I'll be back in a few minutes."

"Why? Can I go with you?" Noah stood up and took a step toward Jack.

"No, you can't go with me. I've got to go into the saloon for a while, but I won't be gone long. You wait for me right there on that bench." He took Noah by the shoulder and steered him back to sit down. "Right there, you hear me?"

Noah slumped against the wall and sat cross-legged on the bench.

Jack stepped into the dusty street and made his way to the saloon. Only a few days ago, he'd come crashing through that window and found Evangeline Gentry standing near the spot where Noah waited for him now. He shook his head and laughed to himself at how things had changed since that day.

He pushed back the swinging saloon doors and walked into the dim, smoky room. In the corner, several men sat at a table playing poker and a plump young woman with a tawdry red dress leaned over a young cowboy. A man wearing a little bowler hat banged on an out-of-tune piano.

Joe, the barkeep, had his back turned, pouring a drink at the counter. Jack walked up to the bar, leaned against it, and slapped his hands on the surface. Joe jumped like a startled rabbit and dropped the glass, sending shards scattering over the floor. His eyes shot up to the big gilded mirror hanging over the counter and saw Jack's reflection. "You again," he sneered as he turned and stepped over to the bar. "What do you mean coming up behind a man like that? I thought Sheriff Dalton had you locked up anyways." He grabbed a broom and started sweeping broken glass.

Jack shrugged innocently. "I just walked in the front door, like everyone else does."

Joe stopped sweeping and slid a hand under the bar to be sure his loaded shotgun was where it was supposed to be.

"Sheriff Dalton released me into the padre's custody. I'll be slaving for Miss Evangeline Gentry for the next few weeks. The reverend calls it doing a service for the community." He took off his hat and casually polished the conchos with his shirtsleeve. "Oh, and by the way, Joe, keep those hands of yours out from under the bar while we're talking."

Joe scowled. "Well, don't think I've forgot you owe me half of the fifty dollars it cost me to replace that window. You should take your lead from that young cowboy Hutchison and pay your debt. I'll be mighty surprised if I ever see a dime from you, though." He turned and started placing freshly washed glasses on the counter behind the bar.

Jack looked up. His dark eyes bored into Joe's back. "If I don't miss my guess, you've already seen about five thousand of my dollars."

Joe set the last glass in place and turned to face Jack. "Come again?"

"You heard me. When I came into this saloon, I had money in my saddlebags. When I got them back at the jail, they were empty. The sheriff says he got them from you, so I figure you might know what happened to my money."

"I don't know a thing about your money. I gave

them saddlebags to the sheriff just like I found them."
Joe picked up a dishtowel and began to dry the same
glass again with nervous enthusiasm.

Suddenly, Joe couldn't meet Jack's eyes. Jack
leaned in a little closer. "I suppose you didn't see
anybody else touch those saddlebags, did you?"

"Nope, I sure didn't. And, come to think of it, I've
only got your word that you even had thousands of
dollars in your saddlebags, now ain't that right?"

Jack reached over and grabbed Joe by his collar,
dragging him halfway across the bar. He fixed Joe with
a fiery gaze, then released him. Joe fell behind the bar
like a limp rag doll.

"It's your lucky day, Joe. As it happens, I'm not
here about my stolen money. I need some cash, and I
need it right away." He pulled the gun from his
waistband. Joe's face turned ashen. He backed away
from the bar and instinctively put his hands in the air.

"Now, I don't have much money here in the saloon,
Brannigan. All I've got is a little cash here behind the
bar…"

Jack threw his head back and roared with laughter.
"I'm not robbing you, Joe." He placed the gun on the
bar and laughed again.

Joe growled at him, "You know you shouldn't draw
a gun that way when you're in a saloon. We get all
kinds in this place."

"Oh, I know you do, Joe. What I want is to sell this
gun." He held it up and caressed it like a sweetheart's
cheek. "This is a brand new, pearl handle, single-action
Army Colt revolver. I'll wager no other man in this
town has one like it."

Joe took it from his hand and examined it, opened

the chamber, and spun it. "It's a nice piece, all right. I might be willing to take it off your hands." He eyed Jack's hat with its silver conchos. "How about that hat? You want to throw it into the deal? I'd give you a fair price for both of them."

Jack shook his head and unconsciously pushed the hat down harder on his head. "Oh no, this hat isn't for sale. Just the gun."

Joe sighed and tilted his head, examining the gun again. "Well, I suppose I could give you a few dollars for it." He drew out the words with a smirk. Jack could see that he thought he was in control.

"How few?"

Joe scratched his chin, looked up at the ceiling, and made a show of pondering how much he'd pay for the gun. "I guess I could take it off your hands for two dollars."

Jack snatched the gun from Joe's hands and stuck it back into his waistband. "I wouldn't let you polish it for less than ten dollars." He turned toward the door.

"Well, hold on a minute, Brannigan – come back here now." He waved Jack over to the bar again. "That is a nice firearm you've got there, and I know you're in dire need of some cash. I'll give you three dollars for it. Take it or leave it."

"I'll leave it. I said ten."

"Alright, alright. Five dollars and that's my final offer."

Jack scowled. "Seven is *my* final offer. Take it or leave it."

Joe sighed. "You got yourself a deal."

Jack placed the gun on the bar and shoved it toward the bartender. "You got yourself a new gun."

Joe took seven silver dollars from the till and handed them to Jack. "You sure you won't change your mind about that hat? I'd give you a pretty penny for it."

"Not on your life."

Jack pocketed the money and turned away but, before he could make it across the room, the door swung open, and in walked Noah. He stood rooted to the floor, taking in the commotion in the loud, smoky room.

Jack ran to him, snatched him by the collar, and pulled him aside. "Noah, what in the world are you doing in here, son? Didn't I tell you to stay put in front of the general store?"

Noah squirmed and escaped Jack's grip. "Yessir, you did but I thought you'd want to know I saw Rusty go into the bank down the street. You ain't supposed to be in town, are you, Jack?" He pulled his collar back into place and re-buttoned the top button.

Jack mumbled something under his breath, but Noah didn't ask him to repeat it.

"Come on. Let's take the back way out of here." He grabbed Noah by his shoulder and propelled him to the back of the bar.

"We're leaving now." He nodded to Joe as they disappeared into the back room.

~

In the bank, Rusty stood in line waiting his turn at the counter. Mr. Dibble was slow as he chatted with a woman about the latest gossip she'd heard in the milliner's shop.

Rusty fidgeted and walked to the window as he waited for the pair to finish their conversation. He scanned the boardwalk across the street, taking note of the new shipment of fishing poles on display in the mercantile window. He thought he might want to stop in and take a look at those poles and maybe pick up a surprise for Rachel. From the corner of his eye, he spotted a white-haired boy and a big man wearing a fancy hat coming from behind the saloon.

Rusty whipped around and headed for the door so fast that he nearly fell over a chair. A wagon passed in front of him as he waited to cross the street. By the time it passed, Jack and Noah had already gone into the mercantile.

Rusty Cunningham's Scottish blood boiled as he tramped into the store and came up behind Jack. "What in blazes are you doing in town, Brannigan?"

Jack turned around and did his best to look surprised to see Rusty standing behind him. "Oh. Why, we just came in for a few supplies. What are you doing here?"

"I'm here because I've got me some business at the bank. But you know good and well you ain't supposed to be in town unless the reverend says so. And you sure as the world ain't supposed to be in a saloon. With a little boy." His eyes blazed.

Jack met his gaze and didn't back down. "Well, Rusty, the reverend wasn't around, and I needed to pick up a few things today. The boy wanted to come along, so I let him. Now if you'll let me finish up my business, we'll be on our way back to the ranch."

Rusty put a hand on Noah's shoulder and pulled him over next to him. "I reckon I'll take this tyke with me. Seems one of us has to be responsible with a little feller this age. I saw where you just came from, and it won't do you no good to deny it."

Jack's expression tightened, but he didn't argue. "Noah, go on with Rusty. I'll meet you both in the bank as soon as I'm done here. Go on, now."

Rusty took the boy by the arm and led him out the door.

After Jack finished at the mercantile, he walked toward the bank to meet Rusty and Noah, a bundle of goods wrapped in brown paper tucked under his arm. He entered the brick building and took a seat in one of the spindle-back chairs next to Noah.

Rusty stood at the teller's window talking to Mr. Dibble.

"Rusty, be sure and tell Miss Gentry that this withdrawal brings her balance down to a minimal amount. I've never seen her account dip this low."

Rusty brushed a hand through his auburn hair. "Well, I reckon she knows what she's doing. She's been wanting to buy new horse breeding stock for quite a while, and she's decided now is the time."

Mr. Dibble lowered his spectacles to the end of his long nose and peered at Rusty over the rims. "Miss Gentry is one of my favorite customers, and I know what a hard time she's had since her husband passed on. She's worked so hard to make a go of that ranch."

"That she has. She works harder than any female I've ever known. Why she can put in a day's work that would put some men to shame."

Mr. Dibble cleared his throat and leaned closer to the window. His high-pitched voice took on an intimate tone. "I think it's such a shame that a lady like Miss

Gentry has to work so hard to make a living while men like Joe Anderson stand behind a bar all day serving whiskey to drunks and they're able to make huge deposits to their bank accounts. Only a few days ago, he made the largest deposit ever. Business must be really good over at the Golden Eagle Saloon."

Jack had been only half listening to the two men talk, but they had his full attention now. He looked up at the banker from under the brim of his hat.

Mr. Dibble looked at Jack. "Oh, that's right, sir. A bag of money. Most of it Double Eagles. It's shameful that a man could get rich from selling liquor."

Jack stood up and without a word, handed his package to Noah. He plowed through the door and tramped across the street, nearly knocking down a man loading his wagon with supplies in front of the general store.

Rusty followed him to the door, yelling after him. "Brannigan, you get back here, now! Don't you go into that saloon!"

He stuffed the cash he'd withdrawn into his vest pocket and took off in hot pursuit of Jack, Noah not far behind.

Jack slammed the double doors of the saloon back. He crossed the room with huge strides, grabbed Joe Anderson by the collar, and dragged him across the bar.

Joe's eyes were enormous, his face pale with fear as he hung like a marionette from Jack's fists. "What are you going to do to me?" His voice cracked. "What did I do? I gave you a fair price for that handgun, didn't I?"

Rusty careened through the doors and grabbed Jack by the shoulder.

"Let him go, Brannigan. Have you gone loco?"

Jack ignored Rusty and shoved the saloonkeeper away. Joe stumbled back against the counter behind the bar.

Jack clenched his teeth. "I knew you did it. I knew you had to be the one who stole my money."

Joe whimpered. "I told you I didn't take your money, Brannigan."

"I was just in the bank, and I heard the teller saying how you made a very large deposit a few days ago, most of it gold Double Eagles. That was my money."

Rusty wedged himself between the two men and pushed Jack away from the cowering barkeeper.

"What's this all about? What money are you talking about, Brannigan? I thought you didn't have a dime."

"I don't have a dime now, but when I came into town, I had over five thousand dollars in poker winnings in my saddlebags. When the sheriff locked me up, those bags were here in the saloon. When I finally got them back, they were empty." He lunged at the barkeep again. "Looks like there's no doubt about who got it, now is there?"

Joe cowered behind Rusty. "You didn't win that money, Brannigan, you stole it. Word gets around at the poker tables, and there was a man in here a few days ago by the name of Dallas Rand. He told everybody how you cheated at a game in St. Louis. He said you had a barmaid signal you on how to place your bets."

Rusty turned to Jack, his hazel eyes blazing. "Well, that don't come as no surprise to me. We knowed what kind of man you were when you showed up at the ranch with Reverend Ingram. I ought to take you straight back to jail right now for breaking the deal you made with him and the sheriff."

Jack fumed. "That's a lie. Dallas Rand is a sore loser. He gambled everything he had and lost, and couldn't admit to himself, or anyone else, that he lost fair and square."

Jack backed away from Rusty and the barkeep. "But you can turn me in to Sheriff Dalton for coming into town if you want to. If you know of somebody else willing to go out to the ranch and do a month's worth of hard labor for Miss Gentry, go right ahead and hire him. But I heard what the banker said about her financial situation right now, so I hope you've got plenty of cash to pay this new hired hand."

Rusty shook his head in disgust and mumbled something unintelligible under his breath. "Looks like you win, Brannigan. But if this happens again, I'll talk to the sheriff. You can count on it."

He started toward the door but turned back. "Noah's waiting outside. I'm taking him with me to drop off this money at Mr. Wainwright's house."

Jack kept his tone even. "I don't think that's a good idea. I promised Noah he could help me with some carpentry I'm doing. The boy just lost his mother. I know keeping busy with his hands will help him heal." He softened his expression. "I'm leaving town now and heading back to the ranch. You don't have to worry about Noah."

Rusty scowled at Jack. "The first day you showed up with the reverend I told you I take care of everything on the Gentry ranch, including Miss Eva. Now that includes the young'uns, too." He took a step closer to Jack. "I don't aim to let you hurt that boy nor teach him any of your bad habits."

Jack stepped closer, and the men stood face to face. "You don't have to worry about that. I don't want to hurt Noah either. You might not believe me, but I'm hoping to teach him some good things. Maybe a couple of skills he can carry with him into manhood. Like I told you, I'm going to show him how to work with wood."

Rusty furrowed his brow, his eyes boring into Jack's. "Just so long as them 'skills' ain't got nothing to do with cards nor saloons." He looked toward the door. "I'll let him go with you only because you promised him, and because I ain't got a lot of time to spend with him myself today. But I'll be keeping tabs on you, Brannigan."

Chapter Eleven

Evangeline sat in the parlor restitching one of her old dresses she had cut down to fit Carrie. A breeze drifted through the open window carrying a clean, fresh scent. She could tell Rusty and the reverend had been dropping hay in the pasture for the horses. The urge to be outside tending to chores was powerful but she knew she had to stay inside with Carrie until the little girl was much stronger.

Restless, she put the dress aside and picked up the letter that had arrived from her mother yesterday. Her eyes went to the passage that troubled her most.

Evangeline, when will you give up the idea of living alone on that little farm with only a few hired hands? Heaven knows how hard you've tried, but it's time you came home to Kentucky and settled down with your family.

Someday, all that your father left behind will be yours. I'm getting older and I want my only child near me.

Alexander Beck still asks about you and, I know if you came home, it wouldn't take long for the two of you to renew your friendship. He's a good man, Evangeline, and has a successful law practice in Lexington. You've been a widow now for over three years. When will you remarry and present me with the grandchildren I long for?

Evangeline refolded the letter and tucked it into the drawer of the table beside her. When indeed? She wanted children as much as her mother wanted grandchildren, but the thought of selling her ranch and moving back to Kentucky, back to Alexander Beck, depressed her. Alexander was a good man, as her mother said in the letter, but she didn't love him.

Mrs. Ingram appeared at the parlor door carrying her silver tea service, a wedding gift she'd brought when she moved from Kentucky.

"I've got tea and cookies. Rachel and I are going to help you with that sewing."

"Oh, Mrs. Ingram, I must have been off in a dream world. I had no idea you were making tea. Thank you. It will be wonderful having help cutting down these old clothes."

Evangeline took her sewing basket from the corner cabinet, passed out supplies to everyone, then sat down in her favorite rocking chair.

Mrs. Ingram took one of Carrie's small, ragged dresses, put it atop an old one of Evangeline's, and started cutting. "You know dear, this is lovely fabric, it'll make a nice church dress when I'm done."

Evangeline took a straight pin from her mouth. "Oh, that dress. My mother brought it to me when she visited last Christmas. It's a pretty thing alright, but a little too frilly for riding horses and mucking stalls. It's a bit too pink and lacy for my taste. It'll make nice little girl clothes, though."

She ripped thread from one of Jared's old shirts. "And the child doesn't have anything. The few dresses she has are already getting too small, and we have nothing for Noah. They both need clothes and shoes."

"This is exactly why we have our Ladies Auxiliary Committee," Mrs. Ingram said. "We'll discuss it at our next meeting and start a clothing drive for these children." She moistened the end of a strand of thread and put it through the eye of her needle.

"Evangeline, the committee meeting will be difficult without you. You're usually the one organizing these drives and rousing the townspeople to give to our causes. Now, I suppose I'll have to depend on Amy Watson to take your place."

Rachel worked at cutting down another of Jared's old shirts for Noah. "That's a good idea, Mrs. Ingram. In the meantime, these things we're making now should get them by."

"And we'll need a few more old sheets for diapers, too," Evangeline said. "Carrie should be almost old enough to start toilet training." She laughed and shook her head as she stitched. "I must admit, diaper changing and washing is my least favorite part of caring for babies, I've certainly learned that."

"I think it would have been my least favorite part, too." Rachel's expression darkened. "If Rusty and I could have children."

Evangeline stopped stitching. "It isn't too late, Rachel. You and Rusty are still young enough to become parents. I've heard of women having babies long after they'd given up. You could still have a little girl with your dark eyes or Rusty's shock of auburn hair. I'd love to see what a child would look like with the combination of your Mexican heritage and Rusty's Scottish."

Rachel raised an eyebrow. "One thing is certain, ours would be a fiery-natured child. It would be nice to hear children calling me mama." She laughed. "You know, my family thought I was crazy when I told them I wanted to marry Rusty. They had expected me to marry the son of one of our neighboring ranchers in Nogales. When they met Rusty, a tall, lanky American cowboy with no pedigreed background, they were about to lock me in the house to keep me away from him." She lowered her eyes. "But Rusty eventually won even them over."

Evangeline smiled. "He does have a way about him!"

Mrs. Ingram dropped her plump hands to her lap. "Be that as it may, I think you'll both have had your fill of diaper changing and the sound of children in the house by the time this is over." She took a sip of her tea. "As a matter of fact, the meeting will probably be the perfect opportunity to make the community aware that these children will need a new family soon."

"Oh. I'm sure I'll never tire of the sound of children in the house," Evangeline murmured, but she felt something close to panic rise in her chest at the mention of the children leaving her home.

~

Jack and Noah galloped down Little Blue Hill and cut across the pasture to the brook near the hay barn. When Jack stopped to let the horses drink, Noah slid down and went to sit on a big rock at the edge of the brook.

"Boy that was fun, Jack," he said, breathless. "I was watching through the door and you nearly cold-cocked that man in the saloon. Can we go back into town tomorrow?"

Jack dismounted and sat down beside Noah. "No, that wasn't fun."

"Yes, it was." Noah laughed and held his fists up in a boxer's pose. "Can you teach me how to fight like that?"

"Noah, I wasn't going to cold-cock the man at the saloon. I just lost my temper there for a minute."

"You sure did." Noah pulled off his boots and stepped into the stream.

"Come back over here, son." He patted the rock beside him and Noah splashed over to sit down.

Jack took a deep breath and looked up at the sky as if waiting for some inspiration. "Noah," he began, "what did your pa do to earn his living?"

"My pa was a farmer and my grandpa, too."

Jack nodded. "He grew food. My pa was a cooper—he made barrels and casks out of wood with his own hands. Both are honorable trades." He squinted at the treetops, searching for words.

"You see, Noah. What I've done for a living for the past several years, is, gamble. I've played poker to make money. And sometimes, I wasn't completely honest when I played." Jack took his hat off and fidgeted with the hatband. He stole a glance at Noah to check his reaction.

"Sometimes I did certain things to, shall we say, improve my odds at getting the winning hand."

"You mean you cheated?"

Jack lowered his head and shrugged. "Well, I – yes, that's right. I cheated. Not always, but some of the time, and that's not something I'm proud of. As a matter of fact, I'm ashamed of it."

He peered at Noah again from the corner of his eye. "Anyway, that's how I ended up at the saloon ready to fight the barkeep. Because I had gambling money in my saddlebags when I rode into town, and he stole it from me." Jack chuckled. "Some might call that divine justice."

"What's divine justice?" Noah asked, his expression serious.

"Well, it's kind of like when you know you're not supposed to eat a cookie before supper, but you sneak one out of the jar anyway. Then on the way out the door, you trip and smash the cookie to pieces. You have to figure it's God's way of keeping you honest."

"Yeah, I see what you mean." Noah swished his toes in the brook and seemed to ponder the things Jack said. "But you don't do that gambling stuff anymore, do you, Jack? Now that God has told you it's not good to make your money by gambling, what kind of work are you gonna do?" His face brightened. "I know, you can make furniture and things with wood like your pa did."

Jack chuckled and wrapped an arm around the boy's shoulder. "I'll give that some serious thought. But for now, we'd better get a little work done on that barn roof or Miss Gentry will hang us both from the nearest tree."

He walked to his horse and pulled out the brown paper bundle he'd bought at the mercantile. "By the way, while I was buying the tools, I picked up something for you."

He tore the paper open and pulled out a pair of shiny black boots. "Here, try these on and see if they fit."

"Tarnation! Brand new boots!" Noah's eyes lit up like it was Christmas morning. He took the boots from Jack's hands and inhaled the new leather smell.

"Well, try them on. If you're going to help me do a man's work around here, you need some good work boots."

Noah jumped down from the rock and dried his wet feet on his pant legs. He slipped his feet into the boots and took a few stiff steps.

"They fit fine, Jack." He walked back and forth looking down at his feet.

"Oh, and there's something else in here for you."

Noah ran to his side and hovered over the open package. Jack pulled a new slingshot and a peppermint stick from the paper.

"Thanks, Jack!" Noah threw his arms around Jack's waist and hugged him hard.

Jack patted him on the back and ruffled his hair. "Come on, let's get some work done on that roof and then go back to the house. I've got a surprise for Carrie, too."

~

Rusty rode into the barn and unsaddled his roan, still fuming about Jack Brannigan. It was bad enough finding him in town when he wasn't supposed to be there, but he had Noah with him in the saloon. The final straw was Jack storming back into the saloon a second time and threatening to pound Joe Anderson into the ground over gambling money.

Rusty could hardly wait to tell Evangeline the truth about this no-account, thieving gambler she was cooking special meals for. Maybe she needed him right now and couldn't afford a new hired hand, but one thing was sure – she'd know beyond a doubt what kind of a man he truly was.

When Rusty left the barn, he heard hoofbeats coming up the driveway. Evangeline galloped up to the barn and reined in sharp.

Rusty looked up at her, a broad smile stretched across his sun-freckled face. "A bobcat on your tail, Miss Eva?" he asked fanning his face with his hat.

Evangeline slid down from the tall filly, the full skirts of her green dress fluttering behind her on the way down. "No, no bobcats around here. I just went to check on the colts and Scarlett was telling me she needed exercise so I took her for a ride."

"Oh, she told you that, did she? Well, I reckon she got exercised real good from the looks of her." Rusty cocked his head to the side and a rumble of laughter rolled from deep in his chest. "Miss Eva, I can't remember ever seeing a woman take care of horses dressed like you are right now."

Evangeline turned to him, a frown creasing her brow. "What? I've ridden in a dress before. A woman can't go around dressed in britches and boots all the time."

She led Scarlett into the barn, unsaddled her, and began working her way down Scarlett's neck with a currycomb. "Did you get the money to Mr. Wainwright today?"

Rusty's smile disappeared and he looked down at

the straw-covered floor. "Yes, Miss Eva, I sure did." He paused and blew out a deep breath. "But there's something I gotta tell you. Mr. Dibble says your bank account is low – lower than it's ever been."

Evangeline slowed her strokes on Scarlett's back. "Yes, I was afraid of that, but I don't want to miss this chance to pick up some good stock for the ranch. I plan to sell horses this fall, so I can replace the money I'm spending now and add a nice chunk." She went back to using brisk strokes on Scarlett. "It's risky business, but if I want to make this ranch grow, I have to take some risks."

"You're right, Miss Eva. It'll take a few years, but it won't be long until this ranch is the size of Wainwright's. I think you're doing the right thing."

She smiled up at her friend. "Thanks, Rusty. You know I do appreciate your opinion. I trust you to help me make these kinds of decisions."

Rusty chuckled. "I ain't never known you to need help making any decision. But thanks."

Evangeline moved to Scarlett's right side and started working with the currycomb.

Rusty patted Scarlett's shoulder, trying to decide how to broach the subject of Jack Brannigan's escapades in town earlier. He took a deep breath. "By the way, Miss Eva, there is something else I need to talk to you about."

"Yes, what is it?" she asked without looking up.

Noah bounded into the barn and interrupted Rusty. "Come on, Miss Eva. Miss Rachel says supper's ready and guess what? Look at these." He strutted over to stand directly in front of Evangeline and pointed down at his feet.

Evangeline put down the currycomb and turned to Noah. "Where on earth did you get those new boots?" She looked at Rusty, who shrugged and shook his head.

"Jack bought 'em for me. Ain't they fine-looking?" He rubbed first one foot on the back of his pant leg, then the other one.

Evangeline lifted an eyebrow in surprise. "Mr. Brannigan bought them for you? When did he do that?"

Rusty cleared his throat. "That's kind of what I wanted to talk to you about. I was about to tell you..."

"Come on, let's go eat supper before Miss Rachel skins us." Noah charged toward the door. "Jack said he has more surprises, too."

Rusty mumbled under his breath, "Yep...he sure does."

Chapter Twelve

The sun dipped behind the blue hills and cast long shadows across the backyard. With supper over and the kitchen cleaned, Rusty and Rachel left for their cabin. Jack smiled as Noah jumped up from the table and ran to his side, no longer able to contain his excitement.

"C'mon Jack, let's give Carrie her surprise now."

Jack scooted his chair back. "Yeah, I suppose it is time."

Evangeline held up a hand. "By the way, did the reverend know you were going into town today? I thought you weren't supposed to leave the ranch without his approval."

"You're right, I'm not supposed to, but I couldn't find him to ask, and I had to buy some things. I made a fast trip into town."

Noah got the brown paper bundle lying on the sideboard. "Yeah, Jack had to buy special tools."

Jack flashed Noah a look warning him to keep quiet.

"Tools? I thought Rusty had every tool known to man out in the tool shed." Evangeline's eyebrows knit together.

"Not quite every one. There were a couple he didn't have, and I needed them." He took the oil lamp from the sideboard, set it in the middle of the table, and struck a match. He replaced the globe and turned it up until it filled the shadowy room with a warm light.

"Jack bought me new boots and this, too." Noah reached into his pocket and pulled out a slingshot.

Jack opened the bundle and took out a rag doll dressed in a red gingham dress and white apron. "This is for Carrie. Do you think she'll like it?"

Evangeline came around the table and reached for the doll, approval registering in her eyes.

"Oh, I'm sure she'll love it. What little girl wouldn't be pleased?" She smiled up at him. "Why don't you give it to Carrie?"

Jack took her by the hand and led her along behind him. "Come on, Miss Eva," he said, using the nickname Noah and Rusty used. "Maybe we can get a smile out of Carrie if we're lucky."

Noah scurried ahead of them and bustled into the bedroom. He hurtled onto the foot of the bed while Evangeline and Jack followed.

Carrie sat up in bed. Evangeline took a seat and scooped her into her lap.

Jack held one hand behind his back and pulled the rocker up beside the bed. "I think Carrie needs something to cheer her up." He pulled the package from behind his back and held it up, making the doll dance on the bed.

Carrie's eyes widened and she laughed out loud, reaching for the doll.

Jack laughed, too, enjoying the game. "Hmm...do you know anyone who likes little dolls with yellow hair?"

Carrie took the doll and kissed it.

"Well, then this must be for you. One more thing." He pulled a peppermint stick from the package and handed it to Evangeline. "I'll let you be the judge of when she can have this."

"I think I'll wait and give it to her tomorrow when I can watch her more closely." Evangeline and Jack left the room while Noah stayed behind with his sister.

~

Evangeline led the way into the parlor and lit the lamp on the long cherry wood table in front of the window. The blue crystal prisms caught the light and cast a soft zig-zag ripple across the wall.

Jack came up behind her and reached around to pull back the curtain that covered the double window. Outside, fireflies blinked and faded in the twilight and a chorus of cicadas warmed up for their evening performance. "Looks like it will be a beautiful night."

Her heart skipped a beat, as it always did when he came near.

She turned to go sit down and Jack gently took her arm. "So, you think the children liked their surprises?"

"They loved them, Jack, I haven't heard Carrie laugh like that since she's been here." She smiled up at him. "You're so wonderful and natural with children. Noah and Carrie adore you."

Jack drew back, his expression becoming dark and distant.

Evangeline frowned. "What's wrong? Have I said something to upset you?"

"No, it isn't that." His voice was soft. "I adore them, too. I'd do anything in the world for those two children."

His hand was still on her arm. "I think they loved your gifts." She lowered her gaze and felt a flush sweep over her. "And I want to thank you, too, Jack. That was such a kind and unexpected gesture on your part."

He stepped in so close she could almost put her head on his shoulder.

"It was my pleasure. They needed something to smile about – even if it's a little thing like a toy." He lowered his head toward her and she could feel his breath in her hair, making her heart beat quicker. "And I think maybe what I enjoyed most was making you smile, too."

Evangeline drew back and stepped around him. She couldn't breathe and needed to put some space between them.

"Let's go outside." She hurried to the door. "I think there's a nice breeze coming up." She stepped onto the front porch and sat down on the rail. Jack went to the edge of the steps looking out across the yard. He unrolled his sleeves and buttoned the cuffs.

"I suppose it's time to call it a night. My bed of hay awaits me." He turned to her and smiled, but it was a melancholy smile.

"Jack, I wish you'd tell me what's bothering you. You seemed so happy a few minutes ago and now it seems something has changed. Can't you tell me about it?"

He nodded. "Alright. Let's go sit down." They moved to the porch swing. Jack sighed and gazed out over the yard, his expression pensive. He couldn't meet

Evangeline's eyes.

"I don't know how to tell you about it really." Jack's voice was so low she could barely hear him. "I guess I've been on the run from myself for the past ten years. And being around these children, especially Noah, has brought back memories of something I've been trying to avoid." He turned and looked at her.

She couldn't be sure in the darkness, but she thought there were tears in his eyes. She wanted to take his hand but didn't.

Jack turned away from her again and sat silent for several moments. He cleared his throat. "You see, after my father died, my mother, Rebecca, married again. She thought he was a good man who'd take care of our family." Jack was quiet again. "But he wasn't good to any of us. He was a drunk and he beat my brother, Jesse, and me. I know he hit my mother, too. I'd often hear her crying at night."

Jack looked down at his hands, balled them into fists, and then opened them. "When the War Between the States broke out, I was sixteen years old. I joined up with my local regiment as fast as I could, to get away from that man." He looked at Evangeline again and smiled a tortured, cynical smile.

"I left my mother and eleven-year-old brother there with a drunken beast of a man. Just walked away from them to fend for themselves."

Evangeline touched his hand. "Jack, you were just a boy, yourself."

He shook his head. "No. I was old enough to know what I was doing. I should have stayed there to protect them, but I left them in that hell hole." He looked down at his hands again. "I heard my stepfather died a few years later. But that doesn't change what I did. I abandoned my mother and brother to an abusive drunk."

"No, Jack," Evangeline whispered, her voice desperate. "You did not abandon them. Don't you dare think that!"

Jack stared out into the darkness of the yard. "Yes, I did, and every time I look at Noah, I remember what I did to my little brother. I'll have to live with that for the rest of my life."

Evangeline gently turned his face to her. "Please, Jack. You must put it behind you. After watching you with the children since you've been here, I know you're a good man."

Jack gave her a sad smile. He shrugged. "Thank you, it means a lot to hear you say that." He took her hand and squeezed it. "I really should be getting out to the barn."

Jack stood and walked to the edge of the porch. He stuffed his hands into his pockets with a heavy sigh. "Good night, Miss Gentry."

She stood and came to him, placing a hand on his shoulder. "You need to forgive yourself. You do no one any favors by holding this against yourself. You only prevent the chance to be a blessing to someone in the future."

He stepped down from the porch and turned back to her. "Goodnight, I'll see you tomorrow."

Evangeline watched Jack stride past the moon-silvered needles of the fir tree in her yard and disappear into the shadows beyond. *Lord, please help him. Help him find a way to forgive himself.*

~

Jack turned over in his bed of hay and rearranged the folded blanket he used for a pillow. He couldn't sleep, and it wasn't the late spring heat keeping him awake. He could still smell Evangeline's hair and see her liquid blue eyes gazing up at him from under thick, dark eyelashes.

And she was much more than a pretty face. The more he came to know her, the more he realized she was a warm, wonderful person. Not only had she taken in the orphaned Suttons, but she had supported him after hearing the most terrible parts of his past.

Even more troubling, the way he kept thinking of things like building baby beds and buying little pink hair ribbons. He'd promised Noah he would teach him about working with wood and how to ride bareback. And he wanted to do those things. Only a week ago, he wouldn't have given a thought to settling down with a woman and children. Somehow, tonight, he couldn't think of anything else.

He gave up trying to sleep and left the barn. The night was still and quiet, save the rustle of the wind blowing through the treetops. Maybe a walk in the night air would settle him down.

He could have walked in any direction but, like a compass to true north, he went straight to the little white house. He knew Evangeline would be sound asleep but he walked to the edge of the yard and sat on the fence rail.

A small, unfamiliar noise broke into his thoughts. Jack listened and heard it again, then took a few steps toward the house. A light came on in Evangeline's bedroom, and soon another light in the kitchen.

Now he recognized the sound – crying child. Maybe Carrie was having a bad dream. He thought about going to the door but didn't want to have to explain why he was in the yard at this time of night. He paced back and forth in the deep shadows of the trees.

The crying grew louder and more urgent. If Carrie merely had a nightmare, Evangeline surely would have calmed her down by now. He paced some more and waited, but the crying didn't stop. Something was wrong. He strode up the back steps and knocked on the door.

Chapter Thirteen

Evangeline walked the kitchen floor with Carrie. An urgent knock came at the back door.

"It's me, Miss Gentry. Is everything okay in there?"

She opened the door, her eyes wide with surprise. "Jack, surely you couldn't hear Carrie all the way down at the barn?"

Jack gave a short laugh, looked down, and rubbed the back of his neck. "No, I wasn't sleeping tonight, and—what's wrong with Carrie? Is it the grippe? Is she getting worse again?"

She let him into the dimly lit kitchen, then went back to bouncing the crying baby on her hip.

"No, she feels cool to the touch. I can't imagine what might be wrong with her but I can't get her quieted down."

Jack took the baby from her and sat down in a chair. He laid Carrie back in his arms, felt her forehead, and looked her over. "What's the matter with you, little one?" He lightly pressed on Carrie's stomach and she quieted for a moment.

"Is it your belly that's giving you so much trouble tonight?" Jack began gently massaging her stomach and Carrie calmed down but continued snuffling.

"Do you have any chamomile tea?" he asked. "And if you have any of that peppermint stick left, I need it, too."

"Yes, but I also have some dried peppermint leaves."

Jack looked up to meet her eyes. "That's even better."

Evangeline stoked the stove and put the kettle on the front burner. After the water was hot, she brewed a weak cup of peppermint tea. Jack gave Carrie sips and then took her to the rocker in the parlor.

Evangeline draped a shawl over her shoulders and curled up in a chair. Jack put Carrie's head on his wide shoulder and rocked. The chair creaked softly as he hummed a familiar tune slightly off-key. Evangeline smiled in spite of herself. She loved the sight of him, big and broad-shouldered, long legs stretched out before him as he rocked in the dainty rocking chair. And she loved the sight of him holding a small child up against his muscular chest, and yet holding her so tenderly.

She cherished the whole scene, but it served as a stark reminder of what she wanted and didn't have. Jack wasn't her husband and would never be – not a man who didn't want to settle down. A man who spent his life wandering the country and gambled for a living.

And these children that she already loved could be taken from her any day if a relative showed up looking for them. *Please, God, don't let that happen.*

Soon Carrie was sound asleep. Jack kissed the top of her head gently and carried her back to bed. Evangeline pulled the sheet over her legs and kissed her cheek. They tiptoed from the bedroom, leaving the door open a crack.

Jack made his way through the dimly lit kitchen to the back door. He stood with his head lowered, not wanting to leave and at the same time, hoping Evangeline wouldn't ask what he had been doing outside her house in the middle of the night. "Well, I'd better get back to the barn; sunrise comes early. Goodnight, Miss Gentry." He put a hand to the doorknob, but before he could turn it, she took him by the arm.

"Wait." She turned him toward her and looked up at him, then looked shyly down at her feet. "Thank you, Jack. I would have walked the floor all night with Carrie, and not known what to do for her."

She glanced up again, as always, a little unnerved by being so near him. "I see your experience with your younger brother has come in handy again."

Jack curled his lips in the faintest of smiles. "I'm glad I could help. Guess it's a good thing I couldn't sleep tonight after all."

She still hadn't taken her hand from his arm and she felt the muscle under his shirtsleeve flex when he turned the doorknob.

"Well, thank you again," she said. "I'll see you in the morning. We're having hotcakes and…"

Unexpectedly, he put a hand to her face and lowered his lips to hers. She caught her breath and stiffened in surprise. "Jack…"

He pulled back and gazed into her eyes with a look she wasn't sure she understood…desire, vulnerability, maybe even love.

"I'm sorry, Evangeline. I didn't mean to..." But he pulled her close and claimed her lips again, this time slow and lingering. Evangeline put her arms around his neck and softened into his chest, returning his kiss with a passion she thought she could never feel for any man but Jared. In that moment, the world around her disappeared and all she knew was the warmth of Jack's lips, the scent of his skin, and the gentle roughness of his hand on her face.

Jack smiled down at her and pushed an errant curl from her forehead. "Forgive me. I'd better go now. Goodnight, Evangeline." He stepped away from her, opened the door, and left her standing alone in the kitchen, reeling with feelings she thought she'd buried years ago.

~

The sun sprawled its beams over the treetops as Evangeline paid an early morning visit to her new quarter horse colts. Breakfast was yet to be cooked, but she'd awakened feeling restless and giddy. She stroked the bay's silky coat and smiled to herself. Jack Brannigan kissed her last night and she hadn't been able to keep her mind on much of anything else since.

She gave the colt one last pat on his neck and started to the chicken coop to gather eggs for breakfast. Rachel was just coming into the yard and Evangeline looked over her shoulder, giving Rachel a radiant smile. "Good morning. I'm getting a late start with the eggs. I'll be inside in a minute."

Rachel gave a short reply and hurried up the steps onto the porch. Evangeline thought how odd it was that

Rachel hadn't even returned her smile. *Maybe she's not feeling well this morning.* She went back to gathering eggs.

In the kitchen, Evangeline put her basket of eggs on the table and washed her hands. "Are you feeling under the weather today, Rachel? You seem a little out of sorts."

"No, I feel fine." She kept her eyes on the skillet of bacon she was frying, still not willing to meet Evangeline's gaze.

"Good. I was getting worried about you." She folded the towel and hung it over the edge of the sink. "I'm going to start a batter for hotcakes. I promised Jack we'd have them for breakfast today." Simply the mention of his name brought a smile to her face.

Rachel turned around and looked at Evangeline. "You have been more than my employer all these years. You've been my good friend. I have to be honest with you about something – about Mr. Brannigan."

Evangeline set her heavy mixing bowl on the table and gave Rachel her full attention. "What is it? What about Mr. Brannigan?"

Rachel drew back a chair and sat down, sucked in a deep breath, and folded her hands on the table but Evangeline found herself too nervous to sit.

Rachel began slowly. "You have not talked to Rusty about his trip to the bank yesterday, have you?"

"Well, I know that he got the money and took it to Mr. Wainwright. Why, is there a problem?" She threw up her hands. "Oh, you mean about my bank account being low. Yes, Rusty mentioned that. It's a little worrisome, but I'm sure I'll be fine." She frowned and tilted her head at Rachel. "But you said this has something to do with Mr. Brannigan. What is it?"

Rachel slowly lifted her eyes. "I hope I am not out of line telling you this."

Evangeline felt dread rising like bitter gall in her throat. "Go on."

"I have noticed you are getting – well, close to Mr. Brannigan." She began to speak rapidly, forcing the words out, her Mexican accent becoming more difficult to understand. "I know you have been alone since Mr. Gentry died and heaven knows there are not many young, available men around this town."

"Rachel, will you please just tell me what you want to say about Mr. Brannigan?"

Rachel sighed. "When Rusty was in town at the bank yesterday, he saw Mr. Brannigan and Noah coming out of the saloon! Can you imagine? I am sure he did not tell you that he had taken Noah into town with him, did he?"

Evangeline wilted down into the chair across the table from Rachel.

"And that is not the worst of it," Rachel continued. "When Rusty ran out of the bank to confront Mr. Brannigan, he did not seem very concerned about having a seven-year-old boy in the saloon, so Rusty took Noah back to the bank with him. Later, Mr. Brannigan came into the bank and sat down with Noah to wait for Rusty." She folded and unfolded her hands and looked at Evangeline to gauge her reaction to what she was saying.

"Mr. Dibble mentioned to Rusty that the saloonkeeper had made a big deposit of gold coins to his account. Mr. Brannigan raced out of the bank and back to the saloon. He attacked the saloonkeeper and accused him of stealing that money from his saddlebags the day he went to jail. The saloonkeeper said that he had heard from a man playing poker that Jack Brannigan stole the money from him in a crooked poker game." Rachel took a breath to steady her voice. She raised her eyes to look directly into Evangeline's. "It appears that Mr. Brannigan is not only a gambler and a barroom brawler, but a thief as well."

"*Rachel!*" They both whipped around to see Rusty standing in the doorway, and Jack directly behind him.

"Rachel, I told you I would speak to Miss Eva about what happened in town yesterday."

Evangeline stood up and looked across Rusty's shoulder into Jack's stricken face. A sick feeling of disbelief washed over her as she remembered how she stood in this very room last night and kissed Jack Brannigan. How she had spent the night sleepless, thinking maybe it was time to trust him, daring even to fantasize about sharing a life with him. This man who had snuck off the ranch, knowing it was against the rules set up by Reverend Ingram, and taken an innocent boy into a seedy saloon. A man whom she now realized was not only a gambler, but a thief. Burning with anger, she took off her apron and tossed it onto the table.

"Rachel, can you finish breakfast? All of a sudden, I've lost my appetite." She shoved past both men and raced down the steps into the yard, tears burning her eyes.

"Miss Eva?" Rusty started to follow but Jack held him back.

"Let me talk to her," Jack said.

"Ain't you done enough damage already, gambler?"

Jack shot a sharp glance at Rusty and ran after Evangeline, who had torn across the yard and into the small horse barn. When he got inside, she was tossing forks of hay to the horses. Seeing him, she was so angry she could have run *him* through with that pitchfork. She looked away and could feel him watching her a moment. Silence stretched between them.

"Evangeline, will you listen to me? Let me explain what happened. Yes, I took Noah into town yesterday and I confronted Joe Anderson about my money. But I didn't cheat in that game. I didn't steal from anyone."

She still couldn't look at him. "Evangeline? Did I give you permission to call me by my given name?" She shoved the pitchfork into the hay with enough force that she heard Jack gasp.

"I'm sorry. I thought we had become close enough that I could call you by your first name."

"Well, you thought wrong. I had a weak moment last night, and I regret what happened between us. I don't know what I was thinking, allowing you into my home in the middle of the night. From now on, I'd appreciate it if you'd stick to the work Rusty assigns you and stay away from us the rest of the time."

She hadn't looked Jack in the eye since he'd come into the barn. She stabbed the stack of hay again and tossed it to the horse in the nearest stall. "You may continue to eat your breakfast and supper with us in the house. And I'll see to it that someone gets your dinner out to you every day, wherever you're working on the ranch."

Jack's voice shook. "So, you won't even listen to me?"

"Listening to you is what got me on the wrong track to begin with, Mr. Brannigan."

Evangeline snapped around to glare at Jack. He clenched his fists and turned toward the door.

"Oh, and Mr. Brannigan. If I ever hear of you taking Noah into a saloon again, I'll send you straight back to Sheriff Dalton."

Jack stormed out of the barn without looking back.

Evangeline sat down on a bench and put her face in her hands, tears coming in hoarse, ragged sobs. *What a fool I am. What a fool to think a man like that could ever be someone who'd settle down and make a life with me. He probably had a good laugh after he left the house last night. What a joke – kissing the prim and proper widow he worked for.*

She wiped her eyes, straightened her back, and walked out of the barn. She strode up the back steps of the house with a new determination.

"Rusty," she said. "Please keep a close eye on Mr. Brannigan today. If he finishes the barn roof, get him started on the main horse barn, maybe find some fence that needs mending, or dead trees that need splitting for firewood. I'm sure you can find some way to keep his shirt wet while he's here for the next two weeks." She left the room and went to wake the children for breakfast.

Rusty's voice carried as she walked down the hallway. "I knowed it was a mistake bringing that man onto this ranch."

Chapter Fourteen

Sunday morning dawned cool and cloudy. Jack woke to the call of a mourning dove nested in the elm outside the barn. The soft cooing of its song sounded as gloomy as he felt.

He folded his arms behind his head and stared up into the shadowed rafters, thinking back to the look on Evangeline's face when she heard about his behavior in town with Noah. Her expression had gone from disbelief, to hurt, and then to anger in a matter of moments.

Since then, she hadn't spoken to him unless necessary, but thankfully, she had allowed Noah to continue to spend time with him. Probably because she knew it took his mind off the death of his mother and grandfather.

Jack had been teaching Noah to ride bareback, and he'd also shown him how to braid a rawhide lariat, Spanish style. Most importantly, they had been working on Carrie's crib. Jack had to admit he was proud of it.

He and Noah had planed the oak, hand-turned the spindles, and sanded them until they were smooth as glass. He had cut the dovetail joints, and they fit together with such precision, he knew the crib would last for generations. Once it was finished, Noah couldn't wait to surprise Evangeline with it.

Jack suddenly remembered it was Sunday morning and Reverend Ingram had warned him to be in church every week while he performed his community service.

He stood up, brushed off the hay that stuck to his pants, and shrugged his shirt on. A hot bath would have been nice, but he grabbed a bar of soap from the top of a wooden crate that served as a washstand and headed to the creek to take a chilly bath before breakfast.

After shaving, Jack put on another of Rusty's old work shirts, the only thing he'd had to wear since someone stole the contents of his saddlebags. His stomach growled and Jack thought about the hot breakfast that would be ready in the house. Sitting at the table and facing all the icy stares every morning got harder and harder to take. He thought about going to the backdoor and asking Rachel to give him his breakfast to eat out on the porch, but immediately rejected the idea. Although he was sorry he'd hurt Evangeline, he knew he hadn't done anything to be ashamed of since being on her ranch. He wasn't going to hide from everyone like a coward.

Jack ran a comb through his hair and pulled on his boots. He heard the door creak open and Rusty's long, slow strides come up behind him. He turned to face him, ready for what he figured would be another unpleasant exchange.

"Morning, Cunningham. What can I do for you?"

Rusty set his big-boned hands on his lean waist and looked down at the floor.

Jack could see something was eating at him, but he seemed to be having a hard time getting to the point.

"What is it, Rusty?" He sat down on an empty crate, cocked his head to one side, and sighed.

"Well, the first thing is Rachel sent me out here to remind you the Reverend is expecting you in church today."

"Yeah, I knew that. I'll be there on time." He narrowed his eyes at Rusty. "What else is on your mind? I can see you've got something stuck in your craw."

Rusty kicked at a nearby stool. "Aw, nothin' I reckon. It's Sunday morning and I ain't going to get into no fight with you." He turned and started to walk away and then spun on his heel and pointed a finger at Jack. "But there is one thing, Brannigan."

Jack chuckled. "Yeah, I kind of thought there might be." He stood up, ready for the confrontation.

Rusty walked back and put a finger in Jack's chest. "Here it is. Miss Eva is more than my boss. I'd say she's even more than a friend. She's kinda like a little sister to me. I've worked for her since she moved out here from Kentucky with her husband, Jared. Me and Rachel helped get her through them dark days after he died. We've watched her go from being a heartbroke little gal to a strong, happy woman who can handle anything life throws at her."

He broke eye contact with Jack and seemed to be searching for the right words. "One of these days the right feller is gonna come along for Miss Eva and, when he does, she'll get married again. When that right feller comes along, I'll walk her down the aisle myself. But, you see, I know you ain't that man, Brannigan." He looked at Jack again, his hazel eyes penetrating.

Jack met his steady gaze. "So, you think there's a real danger that Miss Gentry is going to end up married to me? Is that what you're saying, Cunningham?" The corners of his mouth twitched in amusement.

"No, here's what I'm saying, Brannigan. Miss Eva is lonely, and I've seen the looks passing between the two of you. I know she wants to keep them young'uns, and I know she needs a husband. You don't fit the bill with your fancy clothes and hat and your saddlebags of gambling money."

He stepped in even closer. "I *ain't* gonna let you lead her down the primrose path, gambler. Is that plain enough for ya? Because if it ain't, I can make it plainer."

Jack's fists clenched instinctively and, for a brief moment, he thought about punching Rusty out the barn door and halfway back to the house. Then as suddenly as it came, his anger evaporated and he smiled.

"Yeah, that's plain enough for me. And, don't you worry, I'm not about to hurt Miss Gentry. I know I'm not the kind of man she needs. Any man who's lucky enough to get Evangeline Gentry and those children will have to be somebody special and, believe me, I know it."

Jack walked to the back of the barn, picked up his hat, and put it on. "I'll tell you something else, Rusty, she's lucky to have you looking out for her. When I'm gone, I won't worry about her, knowing she's got you taking care of her and the children."

Rusty's jaw went slack, the fire suddenly gone out of him. He noticed a tarp covering something next to Jack. He walked over and pulled it back, uncovering the gleaming oak crib Jack and Noah had made. "Where in the world did this come from?" He rubbed a hand over the smooth side rails and gave Jack a quizzical look.

Jack shrugged his shoulders. "It's a surprise Noah and I have been working on for Miss Gentry. I know she needs a crib for Carrie, and I wanted to teach Noah a little about woodworking, so we made this together." He looked at the ground. "That's why Noah and I went into town that day. I needed another tool." He looked Rusty in the eye. "But don't tell her about the crib, though. Noah wants to surprise her with it tonight."

~

Evangeline turned her buggy out onto the main road and snapped the reins. Even the horses seemed to sense that today was a special occasion as they tossed their heads and high-stepped toward town. She had awakened feeling like it was Christmas morning. Doc had lifted the quarantine and finally, she and the children were on their way to church. She wore her finest today, and the children were tubbed, scrubbed, and gleaming like new copper pennies. At long last, Carrie got to wear her new pink dress and ribbons. She looked like a princess.

Evangeline took a seat at the front of the church, held Carrie on her lap, and let Noah settle in next to her. Rusty and Rachel had taken seats in the pew a few rows behind. Mrs. Ingram sat at the organ softly playing as the reverend greeted worshippers at the door. Evangeline beamed with pride as Mrs. MacArthur fussed over the children and remarked how handsome they looked in their Sunday best.

A familiar baritone broke through the din of voices in the church and singled itself out to Evangeline. Jack Brannigan had arrived and stood chatting with the reverend. She didn't want to turn around and look, but somehow couldn't stop herself. She craned her head and frowned. A group of young women had formed around him. All the prattling and eyelash-batting made her cringe.

Noah turned and looked at the same time as Evangeline. As soon as he spotted their temporary ranch hand, he leaped to his feet. "There's Jack, Miss Eva. Can I go sit with him?"

"No, you stay here with me, Noah. I want us to sit together today."

"Then can I go ask him to sit with us?"

"No, we'll let Mr. Brannigan find his own seat. And, from the looks of it, you'd have to fight through that pack of women swarming him to get his attention anyway." She turned to the front of the church and stiffened her spine.

Noah continued watching Jack, as though trying to catch his eye and wave him over. Suddenly, his bright smile faded. His eyes soon filled with apprehension.

"What is it, Noah? What's wrong?" Evangeline turned again and spotted a stranger standing at the back of the church.

A man of about thirty years stood near the door scanning the room as if looking for someone. With dirty blond hair, his face was covered with stubble. He wore a torn, filthy coat, despite the warm spring morning. His gaze locked with Noah's. He smiled and came forward. Noah, usually friendly and genial, drew back and sat down so close to Evangeline she could barely move.

"What in the world is wrong, Noah?" She looked up, and the man stood before her, hat in hand, his narrow eyes shifting from one child to another. "Can I help you, sir?" She instinctively drew Carrie closer.

The man smiled broadly, exposing broken yellow teeth. "Why, yes, ma'am." He looked from Noah to Evangeline. "My name's Sutton, Ben Sutton, and I'm so happy to see my brother's young'uns safe and sound. I've been looking for 'em from St. Joe to Hermann and back again ever since I got word my sister-in-law had passed away." He put a hand to his chest and bowed to her. "Thank you, ma'am. Thank you."

Evangeline's heart pounded in her ears. Her mouth went dry. Before she could speak, Reverend Ingram took the podium. "Everyone please stand and sing, 'All Hail the Power of Jesus' Name.'"

Ben Sutton took a place next to Noah and threw an arm around his shoulder in a possessive way that troubled Evangeline. Without thinking, she pulled Carrie so close she started to fuss.

Voices rose in song and Evangeline tried to sing, too, but her voice came out a choked whisper. She turned and looked toward the back of the church. Her eyes locked with Jack's, who'd been watching the whole scene as if he knew exactly what was taking place.

~

Rusty helped Rachel into their buckboard and took his place beside her. He picked up the reins, but sat staring at the heads of the horses and made no move to set them in motion.

Rachel grasped her husband's arm. "I know what's bothering you, *querida*. It is that dirty man who came into the church and sat down with Evangeline and the little ones, isn't it? He has come to take them, I think."

Rusty nodded. "I reckon you're right. That man gave me the willies just lookin' at him. I've got a real bad feelin' about him." He spotted Jack lingering in the churchyard. "Wait right here, hon. I need to have a few words with Brannigan." He squeezed Rachel's hand and strode over to Jack who leaned against a tree, arms crossed and hat pulled low over his eyes.

"You waiting for some kinda invite to the picnic Miss Eva planned for the young'uns, Brannigan?" Rusty asked the question, but he knew Jack was probably waiting for the very same reason as him—to find out what the stranger said to Evangeline and Noah.

Jack chuckled. "No, I'm not expecting any picnic invitations, Cunningham." He stood up straight and nodded toward the white-steepled church. "Maybe you can tell me what that was all about in there. Who was that man that sat down next to Noah? Whoever he was, he upset Miss Gentry and the children, too."

Rusty scratched his jaw and looked toward the door of the church house. "You noticed that, too, did ya? To tell you the truth, I was kinda hoping to kill a little time talking to you until that feller comes out. I want to ask him what he's up to. I ain't never seen the man before, and, judging from the way he grabbed at Noah, I'd say he might be some kinda kin."

"Yeah, that's what I'm afraid of. It's going to be hard to watch the children torn away from her now." He gave Rusty a crooked grin. "She's still not speaking to me, but I intend to make it my business to find out what

I can about that man. If he is a relative, Noah's reaction to him sure was a strange one."

"Looks like you and me finally agree on something, Brannigan."

~

Evangeline emerged from the church grim-faced. Noah clung to her dress tail as if afraid if he let go, he might lose her forever. The pale-haired stranger followed her down the steps and up to her buggy.

"Noah, hold Carrie. And keep both arms around her while I'm driving."

She started to climb aboard, but Ben Sutton took her hand and helped her into the driver's seat.

"Miss Gentry, you and me need to do some talking." He unwound the reins from the brake and handed them to her. He glanced into the back seat and saw the wicker basket. "I see you're planning a little after-church picnic. Maybe I could join you, and we can talk about how soon these young'uns will be ready to pack up and go back to St. Joseph with me." His lips curled into a smile that didn't quite reach his eyes.

Noah spoke up. "Sorry, Uncle Ben, but we didn't pack any extra food."

"Noah!" Evangeline scolded, but it was clear to her that he didn't want his uncle anywhere near them. She wanted a chance to talk to Noah privately about this man who had shown up from nowhere to stake his claim.

Jack came up to stand next to Ben Sutton, followed closely by Rusty. "Mr...?"

"Sutton. Ben Sutton."

Jack extended a hand to the short, grubby man. "I'm Jack Brannigan." He nodded to the tall cowboy behind him. "And say hello to Miss Gentry's ranch foreman, Rusty Cunningham."

Ben glanced from one stern-faced man to the other and shook their hands.

Jack stepped protectively between Ben and the buggy. "Maybe it would be best if you go on back to the hotel and wait for Miss Gentry. I'm sure you aren't in that big a hurry."

Ben rubbed a hand over his stomach. "Well, as it happens, I don't have a room at the hotel. Things have been kinda lean for me the past couple of years, and I'm camped outside of town. I heard Mrs. Gentry has got herself a real nice spread out east of here. I thought maybe I'd stay at her place tonight and take the young'uns back to St. Joe first thing in the morning. I don't have any help back at my homestead, and Noah here looks like he could do a fair day's work."

A knowing glance passed between Jack and Rusty.

"Yeah, I'd sure appreciate it if you could put me up for the night." Ben eyed the team of perfectly matched bays pulling Evangeline's buggy and patted the one nearest him. "I'm sure a lady rancher like you can afford to put up a poor old scratch farmer like me for the night."

Jack grasped Ben's shoulder and propelled him away from the buggy. "Miss Gentry is going to go have that picnic with the children. You, me, and Rusty are going to get a little better acquainted."

Rusty positioned himself on Ben's other side and they started walking away from the church house. Jack looked at Evangeline over his shoulder and nodded his head toward the road. She slapped the horses' backs and they lurched out onto Main Street.

Chapter Fifteen

Pedestrians scattered as Evangeline hurtled down Walnut Street. She careened around the corner and onto the wide dirt road that led east toward her ranch.

Noah gripped the side of his seat with his left hand and held Carrie tight in his right arm. "Slow down, Miss Eva! How come you're driving so fast?"

"Everything's fine, Noah. We're going to the lake to eat our lunch." She slowed the bays to a canter and swiped her windblown hair behind her ears. She looked back at Noah and forced a stiff smile. *Oh, Lord...dear Lord. I'm not ready for this. I knew this day would come, but I didn't expect it so soon. Please help us.*

Evangeline trotted the team for a couple of miles and then turned off the main road onto a narrower one that led south. She followed this lane for another mile or so, feeling better now that they were off the well-traveled road. The lane narrowed more until it was nothing but a path, passable by only one vehicle. To the right was a dense copse of trees and to the left, the hill gently rolled down to a small lake in a glen.

The damp air hung heavy with the scent of green spring foliage and wildflowers. She clicked to the horses. The splashing of water and the staccato sound of the buggy's wheels in the rocky creek bed was loud in her ears.

Her favorite spot to picnic and spend time alone, the place was well hidden from the main road. She needed time to talk to Noah about his uncle showing up. She needed to formulate a plan to keep that detestable man from taking the children to St. Joe.

Evangeline pulled the buggy to a stop and hopped down. "Noah, would you give Carrie to me and get the basket from the back?"

They walked to the shade of a tree, and she spread the blanket. Evangeline sat down and released Carrie into her big brother's care while she unpacked their basket.

"I guess we need to talk about your uncle showing up," she began slowly, keeping her eyes on the basket she was emptying.

"Miss Eva, we're not going with Uncle Ben," Noah stated matter-of-factly.

Evangeline slapped the lid down on the wicker basket. "Believe me, Noah. I don't want you to go with him. I've already talked to a lawyer, but he said that if a close relative showed up to claim you, there would be nothing I could do about it. And, God help me, that's exactly what has happened."

She unwrapped ham sandwiches and dished up plates of the now-tepid potatoes she'd fried, crisp and golden. She smashed a bite of potato for Carrie and spooned it into her mouth.

"Yeah, eat up, Carrie. Who knows when we'll get another good meal?" Noah remarked.

Evangeline didn't look at Noah, her mind racing with other thoughts. Finally, she forced her voice to sound cheerful. "Well, I imagine your aunt will be as good a cook as I am, maybe better."

"What aunt?" Noah asked.

"Your uncle's wife. The one you'll be going to live with."

"He don't got no wife, Miss Eva. Ma always said no woman in her right mind would marry that lazy, no account."

Evangeline stared in disbelief. "What? He doesn't have a wife? You mean he intends to take you and Carrie to live on a farm with no wife to take care of you?"

"If you could call that place a farm," Noah commented.

She looked at Carrie. "That's not possible. Carrie's only a baby. You both need a mother to care for you."

Noah bit into his sandwich and nodded. "Well, it could be he's got another one of them 'cleaning ladies' living with him. Ma said he always liked to bring one of the saloon women in to stay at the house and keep the laundry done." He looked down at his plate.

Evangeline looked from Noah to Carrie, her mouth agape. "Absolutely not," she said, shaking her head with determination. "You most certainly will *not* be living with that foul man and some saloon woman. If that's what Mr. Ben Sutton thinks is going to happen, he's got another think coming!"

Noah peered up at Evangeline, as if waiting to hear how she planned to make sure that didn't happen.

Evangeline stabbed the food on her plate and stared blankly ahead of her. "I guess there's no way around it. I'm a Christian woman, so I can't shoot the man, and I don't see any way of getting him to agree to just go away. It goes against everything in me, but I guess I'll have to hide you and Carrie until I figure a way to get rid of your Uncle Ben. We'll take a train to my mother's place in Kentucky. Your uncle won't find you there."

She set her mouth in determination. "Once we're back in Kentucky I'll hire an army of attorneys, if need be, to keep you and Carrie out of that man's clutches."

Noah grinned wide, then jumped up and cheered. "Yeah, Miss Eva!" He shouted and threw his arms up in excitement. "That's a good idea. Let's eat fast and get going!"

Evangeline's face dropped. "Wait, Noah. It's Sunday and the bank is closed. We'll have to stall your Uncle Ben until tomorrow. Then I'll go to the bank and withdraw our train fare."

~

Jack and Rusty flanked Ben Sutton as they walked him away from the church and the curious onlookers who still lingered, talking in the churchyard. Jack gripped Ben's shoulder with a firm hand and steered him toward the split rail fence near the road.

"Let's stop here and have a talk, Mr. Sutton. Surely you can't be in that big of a rush to head back to – where was it you said you're from – St. Joseph?"

Stopping at the fence, Ben leaned against the middle rail and looked up at the two tall men like a fox cornered by bloodhounds.

Jack rested a boot on the rail next to him and leaned in.

Ben looked from face to face and swallowed hard. "Yeah, that's right. I've got me a small place in St. Joe. It ain't much—not compared to the spread the lady rancher runs, I'm sure."

Rusty got right to the point. "How small? Are you gonna be able to care for these young'uns? Two extra mouths to feed might be kinda hard on you."

Ben swiped a dirty hand across his mouth and stared plaintively at the treetops. He sighed loudly and with much affect. "Yep, it won't be easy. A single man like myself raising two children alone, and me having to work so hard in the field from sun-up to sundown."

He ventured a sideways glance from Rusty to Jack to see if he'd evoked the desired reaction, then went on. "Of course, Nate will be a real help to me. I need an extra pair of hands to do the wood chopping and other chores while I'm in the fields. And I can build a pen for little Carol so he can keep her corralled while he does his chores."

Jack and Rusty looked at each other over the man's head. Rusty's face ashen, he mouthed, "Nate and Carol?"

Jack thought the foreman might pass out cold.

"You mean to tell me you ain't got a wife at home and you still plan to take them young'uns with you? What in tarnation are you thinking, mister?"

Rusty's face was coloring, and Jack thought he'd have to hold him back to keep him from ripping Ben

Sutton's head off. He put a hand on Rusty's arm to calm him down. "Excuse us for a minute, Mr. Sutton. Just sit here and wait. We're not done talking." Jack nodded toward Rusty's wagon and they strode over to where Rachel waited none too patiently.

"What in the world is going on over there?" she asked. "The way the two of you were looking at that man, I thought you were going to hang him from the nearest tree branch."

Rusty took his hat off and slapped it down on the wagon seat. "Can you believe that man? He can't even get their names straight. I say let's take him out to the woods and string him up right now. There ain't nobody gonna miss him back in St. Joe, anyways."

"It's tempting, I'll give you that," Jack agreed. "But maybe we should just give him what he really wants, instead."

Rusty looked at him like he'd lost his mind. "What do you mean, what he really wants?"

"Why, money, of course. He's been dropping hints since we started talking to him." Jack nodded in Ben's direction. "He thinks Evangeline is wealthy, and he's hoping to go home with some cash in his pockets."

Realization crept across Rusty's face. "Danged if you ain't right, Brannigan. You leave that polecat to me. I can take him, even with a busted shoulder."

Jack looked at Sutton, who sat on the fence glaring in their direction. "No. I'd like to handle him the same way, but he's got the law on his side. He can legally take the kids, and whipping him would only get me back inside Sheriff Dalton's jail."

He looked in Sutton's direction again. "I'm going to find out what kind of money it would take to get him to sign away his rights to Noah and Carrie."

Rusty nodded. "Maybe I'd best stick around. I think you might need me to help persuade that feller, if you know what I mean."

"No, Cunningham, keep your hands clean. My name's already mud with Evangeline and the rest of the town anyway, so what do I have to lose?"

"Brannigan, I done told ya. Miss Eva is like family to me, and I ain't about to let anything happen to her."

Jack nodded. "Alright, let's go."

Rusty patted Rachel's hand. "Take the buckboard on home, hon. I'll borrow a horse and be there later."

Jack turned on his heel and walked toward Ben Sutton, his long legs eating the distance in a few quick strides.

Rusty followed close behind.

Jack slapped Ben on the back. "Come on, Sutton, let's take a ride."

Fear flashed across Ben's face. "A ride where? We don't need to go anywhere together. I was thinking I'd go out to Mrs. Gentry's place and wait for her to get home with the young'uns."

"Oh no, we're taking a ride," Jack said, enjoying the apprehension in Ben's eyes. "We have a couple of things to talk over."

Jack nodded in the direction of the horses and waited for Ben to stand up and start walking toward his wagon.

Jack threw a lean, muscled leg over his stallion and then rode up next to Ben's buckboard.

Rusty wordlessly climbed up next to Ben Sutton in the wagon.

Halfway down Walnut Street, Jack reined in and tied Ace to the hitching post in front of the saloon. Ben pulled back on the brake of his wagon and climbed down, followed closely by Rusty.

Jack took a seat on the bench in front of the big, freshly painted window of the Golden Eagle and patted the seat next to him.

Feet dragging, Ben crossed the boardwalk and sat down next to Jack.

Rusty leaned against the hitching post and trained an angry eye on Ben.

Jack leaned forward, put his elbows on his knees, and interlocked his fingers. Moments passed, but he didn't speak.

Ben fidgeted, waiting for one of the other men to say something or make a move. "What the blazes do you want, Brannigan?" He half-rose from the bench. "You said you wanted to talk with me, but you've been sitting here staring at the ground not saying a word since we got here."

Jack sat up straight and turned to look Ben in the eye. "The real question is what do *you* want, Mr. Sutton?" He paused and searched the other man's face. "Do you want two small children who are still half sick? You'll have to feed and clothe them. Then it will be years before either of them can earn their keep."

Ben lowered his gaze and said nothing for a minute. "Well, they are my brother's young'uns. It's my duty to take care of them."

Jack softened his tone. "It's your duty to see to it that they're taken care of, Sutton, and you know they are being taken care of. You know Miss Gentry already loves them and wants to keep them. She'll be sure they're educated, raised in church, and have everything they need. She'll be a mother to them."

Ben looked up sharply. "So, you think I should just let her have them then, is that what you're saying? And if I don't, you and that red-headed, long, drink of water are gonna do what? Beat me into giving away my brother's children?"

Jack chuckled. "I'd be tempted, and I know Rusty would, too but we'll save that as a last resort. We're kind of hoping you'll do the right thing because they are your brother's children, and you want what's best for them."

Ben sighed, scratched his head, and squinted as if in deep thought. "Well, now. I suppose they would be better off with the lady rancher but, the way I figure it, my farm will suffer by not having the boy's help. I mean, who knows how much money I'll be losing by not having his help with harvesting next fall?"

There, he'd said it. Money. Jack knew it was what he'd come for. "Yes, I can see how that might be true. A man like you would probably need – oh, maybe two or three hundred dollars to tide you over until your crop comes in at the end of summer."

He could see Ben pause and look down. When he looked up, Jack knew he had made his decision.

Ben sniffed. "Two or three hundred dollars? Are you kidding me? I could get years of work from Noah after he bulks up and grows a few inches." He shook his head resolutely. "Nope, I wouldn't give them young'uns up for no two hundred dollars."

Jack smiled to himself, happy that Ben had finally admitted he'd let the children go for a price, yet sad he was willing to sell them like chattel.

"So, exactly what would it take to make you give up your rights to the children, Mr. Sutton?"

Ben sucked in a deep breath and lifted his stubbly chin. "Seeing as how Miss Gentry wants my niece and nephew so bad, and seeing as how I'd be losing out on some much-needed help around my place, I don't think I could sign those papers for any less than five thousand dollars."

"You know, Miss Gentry isn't a wealthy woman, despite what you might think. She has her money tied up in horses and cattle and it could take…" he paused for effect, "probably several months to get her hands on any real money."

Ben's face fell as he thought about waiting months. From his expression, he'd already spent the money he planned to get from the wealthy lady rancher.

"Maybe I'd best talk to Miss Gentry herself. Maybe she's got more money than you think she does." Ben stood up and took a step toward his wagon.

Jack grabbed him by the back of his collar and pulled him back down to the bench. "You might want to reconsider that, Mr. Sutton. In fact, I insist you reconsider."

Ben looked into Jack's eyes, black and dangerous. "So, you do plan on making me give up them young'uns whether I want to or not? That's right, ain't it, Brannigan? You and your friend here plan to work me over?"

Jack's laugh was low and humorless. "I'm offering you a little help, that's all. Help to get you through the summer until your crop comes in. And you, Mr. Sutton—you're doing what's best for your brother's children and leaving them with a loving, Christian woman."

Ben straightened his collar and looked up at Jack with fire in his eyes. "Alright. I guess you win. Get me five hundred dollars, and I'll leave town tomorrow."

"I'll give you what I can get my hands on, and you'll leave town tonight." Jack stood up and looked at Rusty. "Keep him right here until I get back. This shouldn't take long."

Chapter Sixteen

Jack pounded on the back door of the Golden Eagle Saloon. He took off his hat and grasped it tightly in his hand, shoved it back on, and pounded on the door again.

Finally, Joe Anderson opened the door tucking his shirttail into his pants.

"What the dickens do you want, Brannigan? It's Sunday, and you know the saloon is closed."

Jack shoved past him and entered the small living space Joe occupied at the back of the saloon. "I'm not here for a drink, Joe. I'm here for money."

Joe sighed and ran a hand through his wiry, uncombed hair. "That again? Haven't we already been through this? I don't have your money."

"Oh, you've got it alright, but that's for another day. I need cash right now, and I don't have time to dicker with you."

Jack took off his hat and lightly buffed the pieces with his shirtsleeve. He fingered them lovingly. "These are my lucky conchos." He looked up at Joe Anderson, a cheerless smile on his face. "Hand-cast, sterling silver." He slid the band off his hat and rubbed it against his shirt, polishing it one last time.

Jack tossed it across the room. The silver coins gleamed as sunlight from the open doorway caught them.

Joe caught the hatband and looked uncertainly at Jack. "You changed your mind? You want to sell this to me?" He grinned and greedily examined the conchos.

"I want five hundred dollars, Joe, and I won't bargain with you. Give me five hundred dollars right now, or give me the hatband."

"Five hundred dollars! Are you crazy? I don't keep that kind of money laying around the saloon on a Sunday."

Jack crossed the room and reached out for the hatband.

"Alright, alright. Just give me a minute."

Jack followed him into the dimly lit barroom and waited while Joe bent down to a small safe behind the bar. The room stank of stale cigar smoke, sour beer, and cheap perfume. It felt like ages since he'd sat in one of these rooms all night drinking and gambling. Had it only been a few weeks?

After a few rotations of the dial, Joe had the safe open. He counted out ten fifty-dollar bills, stood up, and laid the money out on the mahogany bar.

"A mighty steep price, but I've had my eye on these beauties since you rode into town." He grinned and extended his hand to shake on the bargain.

Jack reached out and picked up the money, ignoring Joe's hand. He shoved his plain, unadorned hat back onto his head and leveled a black gaze on Joe that sent shivers down his spine.

Jack snatched a sheet of paper off the bulletin board next to the bar and took the stub of a pencil that hung on a string next to it.

"I'll be back another time to discuss the money you stole from my saddlebags. You can count on that."

~

Jack came around the corner of the saloon and caught sight of Rusty still leaning against the hitching post. He hovered over Ben Sutton like a hawk. Jack pulled Ben to his feet and stuffed a wad of bills into the pocket of his dirty shirt. "There you go, Sutton."

He pulled the sheet of paper from his pocket and quickly wrote a few lines on the page, then handed it to Ben for his signature. "Sign this. It says you give Miss Gentry custody of Noah and Carrie because you can't take care of them yourself. Later, she'll get a lawyer and make it official."

Ben scribbled his name at the bottom of the page and took the money from his pocket. "Four hundred and fifty dollars, huh? Not much, but it'll help, I suppose. And like you said, taking care of that baby would be a big burden on me." He climbed onto his buckboard and tipped his hat. "Been a real pleasure, gentlemen." He slapped the reins and rolled down the street.

Rusty turned to Jack. His jaw dropped in amazement. "Where in blue blazes did you come up with that kind of money, Brannigan? I thought you said somebody stole that gamblin' money of yours. You didn't rob Anderson, did ya?"

Jack started to reply but before he could, Rusty's eyes latched on the plain black hat on Jack's head.

"Well, I'll be... You sold them silver conchos to that snake Anderson, didn't you?" Rusty shook his head slowly, his eyes still glued to the bare hat.

"I gotta hand it to you, Brannigan. I didn't think there was much left in this world that could knock me for a loop, but you done it, mister. Yep, you sure done it."

Flustered and embarrassed, Jack grabbed Ace's reins and leaped onto his back. He looked down at Rusty and pointed a finger at him.

"Don't make a big thing of this, Cunningham. And don't say anything to Evangeline." He turned Ace toward the road. "It was only a hatband. Too flashy for me, anyway."

Jack started to ride away, then turned back to Rusty. "You walking home, Cunningham?"

Rusty chuckled and put his big hands on his hips. "No, I figure I'll borrow a horse from Sheriff Dalton. Why? You offering to let me ride double with you?"

Jack rolled his eyes heavenward and shook his head. "No. I'd rather eat dirt."

Rusty turned toward the jailhouse, but Jack stopped him again. "By the way, can you give me directions to that picnic spot? I'd like to ride on out there and tell Evangeline she can rest easy now."

Rusty frowned and scratched his head. "I don't know. It ain't an easy spot to find. You'd probably miss it even if I drew you a map. You'd best let me get a horse and I'll ride out there with you." He grinned. "Besides, I'd kinda like to see Miss Eva's face when she gets the news that them young'uns ain't going anywhere after all."

~

Ben Sutton pulled his wagon off the road into a grove of trees. He unhitched the team and tethered one of the horses, allowing it to graze on the tender grass. He bridled the other horse, mounted it bareback, and started toward town.

"If them two flunkies think they're gonna get rid of Ben Sutton with a threat and a little wad of money, they got a big surprise coming," he mumbled under his breath. "If I can catch them before they leave town, they'll most likely lead me right to the rich lady rancher."

He rode into the alley behind the saloon and dismounted. Coming around the side of the building, he peeked into the street on the outside chance Jack and Rusty would still be in town.

As luck would have it, at that moment the tall red-headed cowboy came out of the sheriff's office. He mounted the horse hitched out front and rode next to Brannigan.

Ben slid onto the back of his horse and continued down the alley. He'd stay out of sight as long as they were in town, then ride in the trees while following the other two men to Miss Evangeline Gentry.

Chapter Seventeen

Rusty turned off onto the narrow lane that led to the lake.

Jack nudged Ace on ahead and took the lead, splashing noisily through the rocky creek. He was eager to give Evangeline good news.

He spotted her and the children through the trees. Noah launched stones into the water with his new slingshot and Evangeline and Carrie sat under a tree watching him.

Jack kicked Ace, and he bounded out of the water and galloped down the hill to Evangeline and the children.

Noah ran to Jack as soon as he saw him coming.

Evangeline stood up and lifted Carrie to her hip.

Jack tried to read her face, but her expression was like stone. She had barely spoken to him for the past couple of weeks. Jack slid down from Ace's back and walked toward Evangeline.

Noah smiled a greeting and ran to him. His enthusiasm and affection were always plain to see.

Jack couldn't help but wish Evangeline would show a fraction of Noah's warmth.

"Jack, you came to eat with us? Miss Eva, we've still got some food left, don't we?" Noah took Jack by the hand and led him toward the blanket still spread with plates and food.

Jack removed his hat and ran a hand through his hair, his smile waning. "Well, I wouldn't mind joining you, if Miss Eva says it's okay." He looked at her expectantly.

Evangeline opened her mouth to respond when Rusty broke through the tree line. "Rusty's here, too?"

He dismounted and ambled over to stand next to Jack. "Rachel took the wagon home. Me and Brannigan here had a few words with Mr. Sutton."

Evangeline looked from Rusty's face to Jack's. "I can tell something has happened. Which one of you is going to tell me what it was?"

"I think I'll let Brannigan tell you about it," Rusty said. "I just came along to show him where to find you. Truth be told, my shoulder is paining me a bit from all this riding. I think I'll head on home to Rachel. She'll be worried about us by now."

She called after him, "Alright, if you're sure. Tell Rachel we're fine."

Rusty mounted the borrowed horse and turned back toward the creek.

Evangeline appeared nervous, as if fearing Ben Sutton might show up here at the lake.

Jack fumbled with his hat then put his hands behind his back, hoping she wouldn't notice the missing hatband.

"Now what is the news you rode out here to tell me?" Evangeline took a sandwich from the picnic basket. "Is that man gone?"

Jack tossed his hat into the shade of the dogwood tree, not ready to tell Evangeline that he'd sold his prized conchos. He hesitated, suddenly realizing he hadn't prepared his story as to how he came up with payoff money for Ben Sutton.

"Well?" Evangeline handed him the sandwich.

He unwrapped it from its white cotton napkin and sat down.

Evangeline sent Noah to play with Carrie and sat down next to Jack on the blanket. "Okay, tell me what happened with that man after I left. What did you and Rusty say to him?"

Jack sighed and put his food down. "He's not a good man, Evangeline. It would be a big mistake to let Noah and Carrie go with him." His face tightened with anger. "He just wants to use Noah as free labor. God knows what would become of Carrie."

Evangeline put her hands to her face and released a shuddering breath.

Jack touched her shoulder. "It's okay, he's gone. Rusty and I saw to it."

She looked at him, her eyes wet with tears. "He's gone? How did you manage that?" She threw her arms around him. Jack held her close and she pressed her face into the warm crook of his neck. "Thank you, Jack. I don't know what you said to him, and I don't care."

Jack turned her face up to his and wiped away her tears. He cradled her face in his hands and kissed her gently. "Evangeline, as long as I'm here, you and the kids are safe. I'd never let anyone harm you. Don't you trust me?"

She touched his face and looked deep into his eyes. "I want to believe you."

"Then trust me." Those words surprised him as he spoke them. What was he saying? He knew time was short before he had to be in San Francisco for the poker tournament. The tournament that he'd worked and gambled for. The tournament that would bring enough money to secure the future he wanted for himself.

He couldn't tie himself down to this family. And yet the sweet and beautiful face before him bid him stay and the memory of Noah and Carrie's trusting eyes tore at his conscience.

The sharp sound of a twig snapping behind him jerked him back to reality. His body tensed, instincts telling him something was wrong. He suddenly wished he had the gun he sold to Joe Anderson.

Evangeline startled then jumped to her feet.

He stood, putting himself between her and the sound at the edge of the tree line.

About to turn toward the sound, he saw Evangeline look past him, her eyes huge with fear. Jack turned slowly and stared into the muzzle of Ben Sutton's shotgun. "What are you doing here, Sutton?" Anger flooded Jack as he realized Ben had followed him from town. He stepped forward.

Noah came from the lakeshore holding Carrie.

Ben shifted his hand nervously on the stock of his gun, and then wiped a sweaty hand on the leg of his dirty trousers. He took a step closer. "Well, now." He paused, a bit unsure of himself. "I was on my way out of town and I got to thinking. Four hundred and fifty dollars might seem like a good wad of cash but I had to ask myself, Ben, would that buy that parcel of land you've had your eye on? Will it buy a new team of horses and make all the repairs that need doing around your place?" He shook his head. "No sir, it won't, I told myself."

Jack's jaw clenched as the farmer leveraged for more money.

"So, I decided kind of sudden like, to turn right around and come talk to the rich lady rancher myself." Ben eyed Evangeline and grinned. He nodded at Jack. "I know you fancy yourself in charge around here—you and that red-headed ranch foreman, but you ain't married to Miss Gentry. She can make up her mind about how bad she wants to keep these young'uns. No sir, four hundred and fifty dollars just ain't enough to make me ride out of here without my dear brother's young'uns. My own flesh and blood."

Evangeline stepped out from behind Jack. She stared from him to Ben Sutton. "Will someone please tell me exactly what happened after I left the church? What's all this talk about four hundred and fifty dollars?"

Ben spoke up. "Well, missy, this here man of yours took it upon hisself to offer me a piddling wad of cash for Nathan and Carol. Now, I know you own that horse ranch, and I know you've got money. I figure you can make me a whole lot better offer than your man did."

Evangeline balled her fists and lurched at Ben, but Jack put a hand on her shoulder and held her back. She strained against him but couldn't break free. "Now look here, you little mosquito of a man. First of all, this gentleman is not my man." She jerked her thumb in Jack's direction. "And secondly, the names of your dear brother's children are Noah and Carrie, not Nathan and Carol."

Jack tightened his grip on her shoulder.

"Furthermore, I may own a ranch but everything I have is tied up in livestock. I don't have the cash to give you." She turned her attention to Jack. "And what is this about you giving him four hundred and fifty dollars? Where on earth did you get that kind of money?"

Ben pointed the shotgun in the direction of the children. "Get over here, boy, and bring that baby with you."

"No!" Evangeline reached for Noah and snatched Carrie from his arms. "You're not taking these children. You can't have them. You don't love them, and you don't deserve them!" Evangeline pulled Noah up close to her side.

"Well, that's where you're wrong, missy. I can take them, and I aim to do just that."

"I guess it's already slipped your mind that you signed away your rights to these children," Jack said. He took a step closer to Ben.

"That worthless piece of paper?" Ben scoffed. "There ain't no judge in the state that would hold me to that. Especially when I tell him how you and that foreman forced me into it."

He pulled back the hammer on his shotgun and aimed it at Evangeline. "Send them young'uns over here to me."

Noah wrapped his arms around Evangeline's waist. She pressed Carrie tight to her shoulder. "I said you can't have them." Her voice rose, defiant.

Jack stepped between Evangeline and Ben again. "Put that gun down, Sutton. Take the money you got and ride out of here. You'll be making a big mistake if you keep pushing this way."

"Wait!" Evangeline shouted. She put her hand on Jack's arm and pulled him back to her side. "You win, Mr. Sutton. I don't have any money, but if you'd wait until morning, I'll telegraph my mother and have her wire money to me."

Ben grinned and started to lower the gun, then changed his mind. "Now you're being reasonable," he said. "I want another two thousand dollars. That's a measly thousand per young'un."

He waved his gun at Noah. "And I'll keep the boy with me until you get the money."

"No, that won't be necessary," Evangeline said. "Why don't you stay at the ranch tonight? Then you can come into town with me tomorrow while I send the telegram. No need for anyone to have to sleep outside."

Ben considered the logic of her suggestion. "You might be right. I reckon it would be a heap more comfortable sleeping in a bed. And I can keep an eye on the young'uns at the same time."

They were about to head out for Evangeline's ranch when the sound of hooves splashing through the creek distracted them.

Jack sprang forward, grabbed the barrel of Ben's gun, and tossed it aside. Before Ben had a chance to react, Jack drew back a fist and slammed it into Ben's jaw, sending him reeling. Jack leaped onto Ben and pulled him off the ground by his shirt collar, but Ben was out cold.

Rusty slid down from the horse, pulled a lariat from the saddle horn, and tossed it to Jack. "You hogtie that varmint like the low-down swine of a man he is, Brannigan."

Jack tied Ben's hands behind him and heaved him into the back of Evangeline's wagon. "Gladly. And aren't you a sight for sore eyes? What are you doing back here?"

Rusty patted the side of the horse's neck with one hand. "I caught a glimpse of Sutton riding towards this lake while heading out of here. Doubled back as soon as I could, hopin' he couldn't creep up on you."

Jack nodded. "I'm taking him to Sheriff Dalton. Rusty, you may have to give a statement to the sheriff about what happened today."

"I'd be happy to. If the sheriff needs to talk to me, send him on out to the ranch. I'll tell him everything."

Jack picked his hat up from the ground and slapped it against his leg. He pushed his hair back with his left hand and shoved the unadorned hat back on his head. He reached into Ben's coat pocket and snatched out the money he'd given him earlier. "I guess you won't be needing this after all."

Confusion flickered in Evangeline's eyes as they locked onto Jack's unadorned hat. "Jack, your hatband's gone. You must have lost it during the scuffle." She walked back to the grassy area near the trees where he and Ben had come to blows and began searching through the grass and leaves.

Rusty's voice stopped her cold. "You might as well quit lookin', Miss Eva. You won't find it there."

She looked up, her expression puzzled.

Jack shot Rusty a look to keep quiet.

Evangeline took a step towards him. "How do you know it's not here? Do you know what happened to it?"

Rusty stepped away from the wagon where Ben still lay unconscious. He looked from Evangeline's bewildered face to Jack's frustrated one and then back to Evangeline. "I thought Brannigan would have already explained all this."

Evangeline looked at Jack, wringing her hands. "No, he hasn't explained anything."

Jack shook his head slowly and pinched the bridge of his nose, stalling for a moment to decide how to tell Evangeline about the conchos. He laughed and shrugged his shoulders. "It's nothing, really." He jerked his hat off, almost as though angry at it. "I needed money and had nothing left to sell. Why are the two of you making such a big deal over a hatband?"

"That hatband was one of your most prized possessions. You never let it out of your sight." Evangeline glanced at Rusty for confirmation.

Rusty shuffled uneasily and looked at the ground.

"You must have needed money badly." Evangeline almost whispered it. "You paid Sutton off with that money, didn't you?" Her eyes widened in understanding and her voice rose. "Yes, that's exactly what you did, Jack Brannigan! You sold your lucky conchos, and then paid Ben Sutton to leave town. But he got greedy and came back for more."

Evangeline followed his gaze to Rusty and nodded her head. "Yes, that's it. The two of you were together in town. Rusty, you look as sheepish as Jack does." She shouted in exasperation. "Will one of you give me the whole story, or will I have to corner Rachel tomorrow morning to get the real truth?"

Rusty groaned. "Okay, Miss Eva. Here's the dad-blamed truth. Me and Brannigan took Sutton over to have a little talk in front of the Golden Eagle. We tried to reason with him, but that polecat made it plain as day that he wanted cold, hard cash. He don't care one whit about them young'uns."

Rusty absent-mindedly massaged his sore shoulder. "Brannigan knew the only way to get rid of Sutton was to give him what he came here for, so he sold his conchos to Joe Anderson." He gave Jack an apologetic look. "Then Brannigan gave the money to Sutton and made him sign an agreement that you could keep Noah and Carrie."

His words of only a few minutes earlier seemed to hang between them: *"As long as I'm here, you and the children are safe. I'll never let anyone harm you. Don't you trust me?"*

Evangeline seemed mute. She stood motionless, staring into Jack's hesitant face. "Thank you, Jack," she said softly. "I know how much those conchos meant to you."

"They were pieces of metal. I always knew that someday they'd be useful for something more important than decorating my hat."

She crossed the short distance that separated them and put her arms around his neck. Tears slid down her cheeks. "Thank you, Jack. I do trust you."

~

Sheriff Dalton slammed the door shut on Ben Sutton's cell. "I've got to tell you, Miss Gentry, I'm surely glad to know there's nothing left to keep you and them little ones apart."

Evangeline beamed with happiness. "That makes two of us, Sheriff."

"No, that makes four of us, counting me and Rachel." Rusty put a hand on the doorknob. "Sheriff, if you don't mind, I'm gonna take that horse of yours and head on home. Rachel's probably about ready to send a search party after me."

"Go right ahead. I'm sure you'll get it back to me when you get time."

The door closed and Sheriff Dalton clomped across the wooden floor and sat on the edge of his desk. He crossed his arms and focused his attention on Jack and Evangeline.

"Well, I guess this is my day for making folks happy." The sheriff smirked. "Brannigan, I've got some news that I think will make you as happy as Miss Gentry here."

He walked across his office and knelt before a small safe. Jack and Evangeline exchanged quizzical looks as he rotated the dial on the heavy door. In a moment, he had the door open and retrieved a large envelope. He turned back to the two of them, opened the envelope, and pulled out a thick stack of money.

"I intended to bring this to you, Brannigan, but you saved me the trip."

Jack stared at the stack of cash in Sheriff Dalton's hands, his mouth open in amazement. "Is that it? That can't be what I think it is. Is it my money?"

The sheriff chuckled. "Yeah, I figured I could make you stammer."

He tossed the money onto his desk and the stack fell over, cascading across the surface. "After Dibble over at the bank told me about that unusual deposit Joe Anderson made, I did me a little investigating. It didn't take a Pinkerton man to figure out this was your money."

He resumed his position on the edge of his desk. "After I confronted Anderson with the evidence, he cracked like a china doll. Made a full confession." He jerked his thumb toward the corner cell. "He's been locked up nice and secure for hours now."

Jack picked up the stack of cash and flipped through it with his thumb, enjoying the sound and smell of the money in his hands.

Sheriff Dalton paused for effect. "And since you'll have your money back, I 'spose you can pay off the balance of your fine and be on your way." He winked and nodded toward Evangeline. "That is, if you're of a mind to be on your way."

Jack neatly stacked the money and placed it in the envelope as carefully as a man would handle a newborn. "Thank you, Sheriff. I'll take that under advisement."

~

Jack helped Evangeline into the wagon and climbed into the driver's seat. He looked at the sleeping children in the backseat. "I guess this afternoon has been a bit too much for them. They're out like lights."

He slapped the reins and eased the team out into the street. "You've been awfully quiet through all of this, Evangeline. Is everything okay?"

She gave him a faint smile and shook her head. "Yes. I think I'm still trying to absorb all that's happened today. When I woke up this morning, I'd never have dreamed the day would turn out the way it has. I feel like I've been to hell and back all in one day."

He laughed quietly. "I can certainly understand that."

Evangeline mused. "I mean, when I got up this morning, I thought the day would be remarkable only because the children would be making their first visit to church. Then there was the ugly scene with Ben Sutton. And I can't believe that you sold your conchos to make sure the children could stay with me."

She looked up at his shadowed profile. "Jack, I'm so sorry about the way I've treated you these past couple of weeks. I've acted shamefully."

Jack smiled down at her. "You had no reason to completely trust me. And, you know, it was almost worth being treated like a leper to hear the stubborn Miss Gentry say, 'I'm sorry.'"

She playfully punched him in the arm. "But I have to ask you, what on earth will you do with all that money?"

A small voice from the backseat piped up. "Hey, Jack. Now you've got enough money to join that big poker game in California, don't you?"

Jack's spine stiffened. "I thought you were asleep, Noah."

Evangeline looked at Jack, waiting for him to answer Noah's question. He smacked the reins and the horses jolted, sending a spray of dirt and gravel cascading from the wagon wheels.

The seconds ticked away as Evangeline and Noah waited for Jack to say he wasn't interested in going to San Francisco, but he said nothing.

The idea briefly ran through his mind that he could go to the tournament and come back to Evangeline a rich man, but he knew she'd never accept that. Besides, he could still see that big, gleaming white poker palace he'd dreamed about for years.

"Well? Are you still going, Jack? You aren't, are you?"

Jack gave a nervous laugh. "You ask a lot of questions for such a young boy," he said over his shoulder.

They spent the rest of the drive home in silence.

~

Jack drove the surrey into the backyard and pulled up under the shade of an oak tree. "Evangeline, why don't you and the children go on inside? I'll take care of the surrey and the horses." He reached up and put his hands around her waist, helping her down from the buggy.

Evangeline couldn't look him in the face. She straightened her back and went to the house.

Chapter Eighteen

Jack pulled the envelope from his coat pocket. He opened it and thumbed through the stack of bills. Five thousand dollars.

He took the stack of money and tapped it against one palm. He wanted to play in that poker tournament, and he wanted it bad. Part of him still wanted that gambling palace in San Francisco. At the same time, the thought of leaving Evangeline and the children now seemed crazy. He knew the most logical thing to do would be to marry Evangeline and use the money he'd recovered to keep her ranch going. But he wanted to go to that tournament—he wanted it so badly he could taste it.

Jack put his fingers to his temples and shook his head in helplessness. He gazed up into the rafters and hoped some revelation would come to him. He wanted to make her listen. But listen to what? He wasn't sure, himself, what he wanted to say. "Face it, Brannigan. You want to have your cake and eat it, too."

"Are you and Miss Eva done fighting?" Noah poked his head in the barn door.

"Fighting? What makes you think we were fighting?"

Noah shrugged his shoulders and looked away. "Are you coming in to eat? Miss Rachel said supper's almost ready."

Jack looked at the floor. "Not right now, Noah. I've got some things to do." He tousled the boy's hair. "But I think we should give Miss Eva the crib tonight. After supper, you come on out and help me carry it into the house. What do you think of that idea?"

"Yessir, Jack! That's a great idea. Don't worry, I won't say a word. It'll be the biggest surprise she's ever had!"

~

Jack leaned into the jamb of the wide barn door as evening fell. Behind him, the horses nickered and made rustling noises as they munched on fresh hay. Outside, the night bugs started their evening chant.

He could hear voices from the kitchen—Evangeline and Rusty talking, Rachel laughing at something they'd said and Noah, loud and excited as usual.

Finally, the lamp went out in the kitchen, and he saw Rusty and Rachel come outside. Rachel said something to Rusty, and he rode away as she took the path to their cabin. Jack knew it would only be minutes before Noah came through the door to help him take the crib into the house. Soon the back door opened, and he heard Noah's footsteps hurrying through the gravel.

"Jack." Noah poked his head into the barn. "Are you ready? Let's get this done before Miss Eva comes outside looking for me.

Jack chuckled. "Okay, Noah, let's get the crib inside, and I'll make sure you get most of the credit." He threw back the tarp that covered the pale oak bed and dragged it out from the wall. "Are you sure you can carry your end? This thing is pretty heavy."

Noah looked stricken. "You just worry about your end, Jack. I'll get my half up the stairs okay."

Jack threw his head back and laughed. "Okay, squirt. Let's get it into the house."

Noah huffed and puffed as he topped the last step and set his end of the crib on the back porch.

"Wait a minute." Jack wiped his hands on his pants legs. "Let me get the screen door open. Now, remember, try to be real quiet going into the kitchen."

"I will, Jack. But hurry."

After what seemed a long, slow struggle, they finally had the crib in the dark kitchen.

"Okay, go get her," Jack whispered. "It sounds like she's out on the front porch." He watched as Noah scampered off to get Evangeline. He followed as far as the sitting room door and waited there. The moon cast shadows through the curtain much as it had that first night he saw her rocking Carrie by the window. That had only been a month ago, and yet so much had changed during that short time.

Jack had the money now to pay off his fine, and he was free to go where he pleased. Free to continue to California and pursue his dream of owning a gambling palace. Tomorrow he'd be on his way, so why did he feel so miserable about leaving?

Evangeline followed Noah into the house, one hand over her eyes. He held her other hand and led her across the carpeted floor. "Careful, Miss Eva. Don't run into the chair."

She giggled and took smaller steps. "What in the world is this big surprise you have for me?"

"You'll see. It's right here in the kitchen." He led her through the door and stopped by the table. "Okay, open your eyes."

~

Evangeline opened her eyes and looked across the table, straight into the face of Jack Brannigan. He wore a small, unreadable smile. His gaze met hers, and she felt the same rush of blood to her cheeks she'd felt when he came into the room that very first night. Her pulse quickened as it did every time she saw him or heard his voice from another room.

"Well, what do you think, Miss Eva?"

Noah's words pulled her back to the here and now.

Jack stepped aside with a flourish.

Her eyes widened. "Oh my, what a beautiful crib! Where did this come from?"

"We made it, Miss Eva. Me and Jack. We've been working on it out in the barn. That's why we had to go into town that day – so Jack could sell his gun. We had to buy a hand lafe."

"A hand lathe," Jack corrected.

She went to the crib and ran her hand over the smooth, highly polished wood.

"I hope you don't mind. This is the reason I wanted to use the oak I found in the hay barn." Jack's voice was soft.

Tears welled up in her eyes and she threw her arms around Noah. "This is the most beautiful thing I've ever seen," she said. "You've done a fine job."

"And Jack, too." He beamed up at her and then at Jack. "He showed me how to do it and helped a little, too."

Jack winked at him.

Evangeline swiped tears from her cheeks. She wanted to draw Jack into her embrace and tell him how much she loved the crib. How much it meant to her that the two men she loved most in the world had crafted it with their own hands. "Carrie is going to love this, too." She hugged Noah tighter and looked over his head at Jack. The look on his face was so tender. How could she be angry with him? Then she reminded herself that he was leaving come morning because he couldn't commit to them.

Jack clapped his hands together. "Well, let's get this moved into the bedroom."

"Oh, no. We'll wake Carrie up if we move it now. It can wait till morning. I need to make a mattress for it, anyway."

"I was planning on hitting the road about dawn." He couldn't meet her stare.

Noah shot him a confused glance. "Leaving? You're still going to California, Jack?"

Evangeline felt something close to panic rise in her chest. "Could I have a word with you? Maybe you'd go out on the front porch with me."

Jack rubbed his jaw and hesitated. For a moment, she thought he'd say no, but he nodded and put a hand on the small of her back, directing her out of the kitchen.

"We'll be outside." She shot Noah a look over her shoulder. "You should start getting ready for bed."

In the short distance between the kitchen and the front porch, Evangeline came to a decision. She wasn't going to be the angry, stubborn woman she'd been with Jack for the last month. She loved him, and she wanted him to know it before he left her forever.

The nearly-full moon peeked through the treetops and cast a faint light on the porch. So many things about this night reminded her of the first night he came to the ranch. That night was the beginning, but she didn't want tonight to be the end.

He stood behind her as she took a handkerchief from her pocket and nervously twisted it. She looked out across the yard, trying to find the words to tell him what she felt. "Jack, I need to tell you something before you go. I...I don't think I've ever really said thank you for everything you've done for us." She glanced up at him over her shoulder.

"I know being here the last month was not by your choice, but you've done so very much for me and the children - more than you had to. You sold some of your most precious possessions to help us. You sold your conchos to pay off Mr. Sutton, and, only a few minutes ago, Noah let it slip that you sold your gun so you could both make the crib for Carrie."

The oak branches swayed in the breeze and made a soothing sound. She kept her back turned to Jack, unable to look him in the eye. He still hadn't said a word, but she continued. "You've helped a little boy through the grief of losing his mother and been more than a friend to him."

She finally turned and looked up into his face. "Thank you for everything, Jack," she whispered. "And...and I have to tell you before it's too late. I've come to..." she choked on the words, afraid she'd make a fool of herself, but determined to tell him.

Jack cupped her chin and leaned closer to her. "You've come to what, Evangeline?" When she tried to turn her face away, he held it still. "What were you going to say?"

"I was going to say that I love you and so do the children." She squeezed her eyes tightly shut, and the words came out in a rush lest she lose her nerve. "I may be the world's biggest fool for saying it, but it's true. When you first came to the ranch, I thought you were an insufferable, arrogant cad, but I've come to see you for the kind, loving, strong man that you are and, God help me, I'm going to miss you terribly when you leave. You'll leave a hole in our lives that no one else will be able to fill."

He put his lips to her ear and whispered, "I love you, too Evangeline. I love you and those children inside." He kissed her ear softly. "And if you'd given me half a chance, I'd have told you so by now."

He took her face in his hands and kissed her.

She rested her head on his shoulder. "Jack, I've been so confused. You hesitated when Noah asked you if you were going to California. You couldn't give us an answer. I thought you wouldn't want to settle down – that gambling was more important to you than family."

"Nothing is more important to me than family, Evangeline." He brushed a stray curl back from her forehead. "I think I told you once that when I found the right woman, I'd be ready and able to take care of a family."

"That seems like such a long time ago – that day we ate fried chicken in the glen." A laugh bubbled from her lips. She searched his face. "And have you found the right woman? One you love more than a gambling palace?"

Jack inhaled deeply and looked up toward the stars. He blew out his breath in an audible sigh. "Evangeline, I love you more than anything in the world that money can buy. I know that now. But..."

She froze.

"Giving up on a dream isn't that easy. And making a lifetime commitment isn't easy either." He looked her in the eye. "I love you and I want to be with you and the children forever, if you'll have me. But there's something I need to do first."

Her heart shattered at his words. She had been sure he was about to tell her he wanted to stay, marry her, and make a family with her and the children.

"Something you need to do first? What? Do you mean you are still going to San Francisco?"

"Yes, if I win that..."

She stopped him short, her temper flaring. "On no, Jack Brannigan. No, we won't wait while you go over a thousand miles away and enter a gambling tournament in hopes of winning more money. What if you change your mind and don't even come back? Do you know what that would do to Noah?"

"I won't change my mind."

She jerked away from him. "Just go, Jack. Go play your game – fulfill your dream. Only don't bother coming back to us when you've had your fun. We won't be waiting for you."

She was furious—hurt and furious. This was the second time Jack disappointed her. She whirled around at him. "In fact, the more I think about it, the more I realize that we really aren't compatible at all." She walked a few steps away from him and coolly turned back to him. "I'm sorry, Jack, I've been living in a dream world. I'm glad this happened tonight. Since Jared died, I've been much lonelier than I realized. Having you here has made me understand that. But now I know that you and I are two completely different types of people, cut from different cloth. Things could never have worked out between us."

From his expression, her words had landed like a slap to Jack's face. "Well, thank you for making yourself so clear to me, Miss Gentry." Jack's tone was cold and clipped. "I guess we both got a little caught up in something that could never be."

She plastered a false smile on her face. I can't let myself fall apart in front of him. Words rushed forth. "Please don't misunderstand, Jack. I'm eternally grateful for all you've done for us, but it's better that we both face reality right here and now."

He stepped in close to her again and gently squeezed her shoulder. "You're right, of course. Thank you for everything, Evangeline. Please take care of yourself and those wonderful children. I'll be on my way first thing in the morning." He turned and walked through the yard and back to the barn.

Evangeline put her hands over her eyes and cried bitterly. "Goodbye, Jack. If only things could have turned out differently."

~

The moon was fully risen and the sound of cicadas and the wind in the treetops seemed louder than usual. Jack couldn't sleep. Evangeline's angry words kept him awake. Why wouldn't she listen? Why didn't she trust him to come back to her and the children?

There was a heaviness in the air, and he wondered if

a storm was heading their way. He stooped to pick up his bedroll and sleep outside under the trees when the sound of pounding hoofbeats made him rush out of the barn. Chester commenced barking and ran alongside the rider.

Rusty reined in sharply and slid down from his horse.

"What the devil is going on?" Jack asked. "What are you doing out in the middle of the night?"

Rusty swiped a sleeve over his sweaty forehead and turned a look on Jack that made his blood run cold.

"What is it, Cunningham? What's happened?"

"I just come from Independence. Miss Eva had me go into town this evening to see if Zeke and Charlie had met up with Wainwright about that breeding stock. They've been gone too long already."

Rusty looked away from Jack and shook his head. "I found 'em alright. I found 'em at the Golden Eagle along with Sheriff Dalton and a couple of other ranchers from around here."

He turned back to Jack with a fearsome look of anger. "It's all gone, Brannigan."

"What?" Jack became more alarmed by the moment. "What's all gone?"

"Miss Eva's money," he said quietly. "All that money she sent with Wainwright to buy breeding stock. All the money she has in the world...it's all gone. Miss Eva is flat broke now."

"What are you talking about, Cunningham? How can she be broke?"

Rusty sighed and his shoulders sagged. "When I went into town to try and find out what was taking Zeke and Charlie so long, I could hear a ruckus at the Golden

Eagle, and I don't mean the usual drunks getting rowdy. I went in to see if they might be having a drink before heading back here with the horses and sure enough, they was in there. Sheriff Dalton was telling the boys and them other ranchers how he'd just got a telegram from Abilene. It appears Wainwright never bought the horses. Seems like he skipped out with everyone's money and ain't been seen by nobody since."

Jack swiped a hand across his stubbly face and groaned. "So that was all of it? All the money she had?"

"Yep." Rusty snatched his hat off his head. "I was a little nervous about her draining her bank account to invest in breeding stock. Now, she's in some serious money trouble."

"Well, what is Dalton going to do about this? Is the law in Kansas after Wainwright?"

"Oh yeah, supposedly, but I ain't holding out much hope of Miss Eva ever getting any of her money back."

Anger simmered in Jack's veins. "First Ben Sutton, now this." He ran a hand through his shock of uncombed hair. "Well, I don't know about you, Cunningham, but I'm going after Wainwright. He's not getting away with this."

"Let the state authorities handle it, Brannigan. They know what they're doing." Rusty's voice softened. "So, you're really leaving tomorrow? After everything you've been through with Miss Eva, you're leaving?"

Jack rubbed his hands over his eyes. His heart wrenched at the thought of riding away from this family when they needed him so much. He shook his head. "I don't want to, but..." He stopped short. "It's complicated."

"Listen. I know you care about Miss Eva. You've

proved that beyond a doubt. But if you don't want to settle down and be the man she needs, you need to ride on out of here tomorrow like you planned. She'll forget about you in time and meet a man that can put her and the young'uns first."

Jack opened his mouth to say something rude but stopped. "It isn't a matter of what I want anymore. Evangeline wants me gone, and she's made that clear." He shook his head. "I just wish there was something I could do to help her before I go."

Rusty stepped in closer and held out his hand to Jack. "I know we didn't start on the best of terms, but...well, you've showed yourself to be a feller I'd go into any battle with."

Jack shook his hand knowing Rusty had given him the highest possible praise. "You know something, I'd fight by your side, too, Cunningham."

Chapter Nineteen

Jack stuffed his saddlebags with his meager possessions, the few dollars he had left from the sale of his conchos, and enough beans and jerky to last a few days. He checked his bedroll and put his rain slicker within easy reach, knowing he'd probably need it soon.

He'd come to a decision after talking to Rusty the night before and learning that Evangeline lost all her money. Jack took the envelope of money Sheriff Dalton returned to him and pulled the stub of a pencil he'd grabbed from the saloon. He wrote on the envelope.

My dearest Evangeline,

I hope someday you can forgive me for being such a disappointment to you and the children. And I hope this money will help you get back on your feet after the loss you suffered at Wainwright's hands.

I do love you and the children. I'll miss you more than you can ever know.

Jack

He propped the envelope against the basin on his makeshift washstand and turned away. The barn door screeched open and Jack turned to see Noah standing in the doorway. "Come on in, son," he said.

Noah sauntered across the barn and took a harness from the wall, in a nonchalant manner. "Miss Eva asked me to take a look at this for her." The boy couldn't meet his gaze. "She thinks it's about to break."

"Oh, I see." Jack patted Ace on his rump and sat down on a nearby stool. "Noah, come here."

Noah stiffened and continued his inspection of the harness.

"Come here, son." Jack's tone was gentle.

Noah dropped the harness and went to stand in front of the stool. "What is it?" he asked, his arms folded tight across his chest.

Jack put a hand on Noah's shoulder, but he jerked away. "I guess you're pretty angry with me, aren't you?"

"No, I ain't angry. Why should I be angry?" Noah looked up at the rafters and made a valiant effort to hold back tears. "Just 'cause you said you were gonna teach me to ride Ace bareback, and you was gonna make a rope swing by the pond. But you're leaving instead." Tears betrayed him and streamed down his freckled cheeks.

Jack grabbed him and pulled him close. "I know it, son. I know I promised – but I can't stay any longer. I have to go."

"Why?" Noah's voice was hoarse with emotion. "You could stay if you wanted to."

"No, I can't. Miss Gentry's had enough of me, and it's making her unhappy having me around the place." Jack felt his heart ripped to shreds. He knew how much he was hurting Noah, and it tore him up inside.

Noah jerked away from him. "You could stay if you wanted to. You and Miss Eva could get married, and we could be a family if you wanted to. But go on, get out of here. We don't care –go on and leave." He ran from the barn and disappeared from sight.

Jack put his hands to his eyes and forced back blistering tears of his own. Oh, if only things were that simple.

He shoved his hat on, mounted Ace, and kicked his sides so hard the stallion reared and bolted from the barn. They tore across the yard, chunks of turf flying behind them as they raced out onto the tree-covered lane. Jack didn't look back. He couldn't.

~

Evangeline watched from the kitchen window as Noah ran from the barn and Jack rode away. *He's gone. Oh, Lord, please help me. Please help me to be strong. Help me to be thankful for the blessing You've given me by allowing these beautiful children into my life. And help me to forget Jack Brannigan.*

Half an hour later, Evangeline stood on the back porch watching the storm clouds roll in from the northeast. The wind whipped the tree branches in every direction and a strong gust hit Evangeline, causing her to grab the newel post to keep her balance. "Noah, this storm will be here any time now. You'd better bring in a good supply of wood before the rain hits. I need to start bread soon."

"Yes, Miss Eva. Come on, Chester, let's go." Noah ran out to the woodpile and loaded his arms with firewood. The trail Jack had taken toward the river lay beyond the fence. Maybe, if he hurried, he could catch him before he got too far away. Noah dropped the firewood and headed for the path toward the river with Chester at his heels.

~

Jack followed the Little Blue River east toward Sibley where it would meet up with the Missouri River. At that point, he would board a riverboat and go back to St. Louis. From there his plans weren't clear. He thought maybe he'd travel south to New Orleans and try his luck there.

Despite everything he could do, his thoughts kept returning to the little white house under the giant oak tree. He could see the rocking chair that sat under the front window and the green ferns swinging in the breeze.

Evangeline's face wouldn't leave him alone. In his imagination she stood on the porch with her hair in a riot about her face, her sapphire eyes filled with life and humor. Since the night he came into her house and saw her rocking Carrie in the moonlight, he'd known he loved her. It had taken him a while to admit it, but he knew. Later when he'd kissed her, his heart had blazed up like dry tinder.

And the children. He wondered how she'd raise those children alone. Noah was going to be a handful, especially now that he was almost eight years old and angry at the world. Jack knew he had contributed more than his share to the anger Noah carried. He'd broken promises to the boy and let him down, the same way he'd let Jesse down all those years ago. Children need protection, and Jack had failed at protecting everyone he'd ever loved, even his own family.

A streak of lightning split the sky, followed by a boom of thunder that echoed across the valley. Rain began to pelt him, stinging the back of his neck like tiny needle pricks. He pulled his hat lower and his collar higher and slowed Ace to a walk. The trail would soon be slick with mud. He was in no hurry anyway.

A somber mood enveloped him as he rode through the rain. A few weeks ago, he would have been excited about riding the riverboats, making his next killing at the poker tables. Now, he was a changed man – a man whose heartstrings were pulled by a bad-tempered lady rancher and two blond orphans.

The rain came harder still, so he thought he should find an overhang and wait out the storm, but he kept going. With every step Ace took, a feeling of foreboding grew stronger in Jack. Something was wrong at the ranch; he could feel it in his gut. Maybe he should turn around and go back. But what would he say to Evangeline? And going back meant he'd have to say goodbye to the children all over again. Maybe his imagination was playing tricks on him because he missed them already.

Jack pulled Ace up under a tree and sat for a moment willing himself to stay calm. He pulled his slicker from his bedroll and put it on. He sat under the tree with the wind and rain growing more violent with every passing minute, not trusting his feelings.

He turned Ace back onto the trail and trudged forward through the slick mud when a scripture he'd memorized years ago rang in his head. *Trust in the Lord with all thine heart; and lean not unto thine own understanding. In all thy ways acknowledge him, and he shall direct thy paths.*

Ace whinnied and rolled his eyes, then reared wildly, almost throwing Jack. As he struggled to regain control, he looked down at the trail and saw a copperhead slither down the bank and under a rock. His premonition of danger – his feeling that something was wrong with Evangeline or one of the children – was so intense he could fight it no longer. Jack turned his mount around and started back toward the ranch as fast as he could go.

Lord, it's been a while but I'm talking to You now and I hope You're listening. I don't know what's going on at home but, whatever is, I pray that You'll protect that little family. Please, God, help me get there in time to help them.

~

As Evangeline ran inside from the root cellar, the rain pelted in the kitchen window. She lowered it and hurried into Carrie's bedroom to put the eastern window down.

Where is that boy? He should have been back with that wood by now. She picked Carrie up and sat her in her beautiful new crib and started back toward the kitchen door. Pulling on a shawl, she stepped out onto the back porch. "Noah!" she shouted. "Noah!"

She scanned the backyard and saw him nowhere. Thinking he may have gone into the barn for something, she pulled the shawl up over her head and slogged across the yard.

"Noah?" She stepped into the barn expecting to find him there, but he wasn't inside. Suddenly her eyes fell upon the envelope leaning against Jack's washbasin. She took a few steps closer, feeling some inexplicable apprehension about what it might be. Surely, he had said everything that needed to be said.

She picked up the envelope and read the note Jack had written on the front, tears welling up in her eyes. She opened it and gasped as she pulled out the contents. Jack's money – five thousand dollars. "No Jack. Oh, no, I can't believe you've done this!" She stuffed the envelope under her shawl and ran from the barn, sliding in the now muddy yard.

She ran through the backdoor and into the kitchen, snatching up her shotgun. Stepping back out onto the porch, she fired off one shot as a signal to Rusty that something was wrong.

Within minutes, Rusty appeared in the kitchen with Rachel close behind. "What in the world's going on, Miss Eva? I nearly slid most of the way down the hill in that mud."

Looking over Rusty's shoulder, Rachel's face pulled into a small frown. She moved in close and put her hands on Evangeline's shoulders. "What is it, Evangeline? Something's wrong, I know it."

Evangeline shook her head and held out the envelope. "I can't believe it. Jack left all his money here...for me! I simply don't understand it! And besides that, I can't find Noah. Why is he out lollygagging in this storm?"

Rusty took the envelope and thumbed through the money inside. A slow smile crossed his face. "You know, I ain't surprised at him doing something like this. I ain't a bit surprised."

Evangeline looked at Rusty in amazement. "Well,

I'm surprised! Why would he do something like this?" Her voice rose as she became even more agitated. "Why would he leave all his precious 'gambling palace' money and yet ride away from those who – who love him." She broke down in tears and turned away, embarrassed at her show of emotion and the admission she'd made in front of Rusty and Rachel.

Rusty turned her around to face him. "Don't be ashamed of it, Miss Eva. Love's nothing to be ashamed of."

Stubbornness crossed her face again. "It doesn't matter anyway. What do we really have in common?"

"How about a love for them two orphan kids and a love for each other?"

She looked up at Rusty and tears slid down her face. "Then why did he leave us?" Her voice was low and hoarse.

Rusty shuffled his feet and cleared his throat. He paused a moment, then said, "Miss Eva, you know you're like a sister to me."

Her face tensed up at Rusty's change of attitude. "Yes," she said slowly.

"Well, don't you think maybe that's it? Stop and think about what you just said right there. The man has done you a lot of kindnesses since he's been here, and think about the way you talked about him. Stop and think through all the things you've said about him since he's been here. I wouldn't be at all surprised if he didn't believe that you think you're a little too good for him. And if he didn't think that you'd never be able to forgive the mistakes he's made in his past."

Rusty's eyes landed on the envelope. "The man just left you every cent he has in the world, and you want to reject it. That's like rejecting the man hisself."

Realization crept through her. Her shoulders slumped and she stumbled to the kitchen table and fell into a chair. "What a fool I've been. What a 'holier than thou' fool."

Rusty came over and sat down next to her. "No, Miss Eva, you ain't no fool. You're one of the finest women I've ever known." He reached over and touched her shoulder lightly. "But you expect so much of yourself, and you maybe expect a little too much of others sometimes." He spoke more softly now. "A man might think he couldn't live up to your high standards."

She wiped the tears as they flowed freely. "Why do I always seem to learn these lessons when it's too late?"

Rachel took Evangeline's hand. "It isn't too late— it's never too late. You said this to me not very long ago. 'Cast your care upon Him for He cares for you.' You taught me that all good things work together for those who love God." She put her arms around Evangeline's shoulders. "Don't give up on anything. Just pray and wait."

Evangeline stood up and hugged Rachel tightly. "Thank God for friends like you and Rusty."

Lightning flashed, followed by a roll of thunder. "Where is Noah?" Rachel asked. "He can't be playing around in this storm." She looked out the back window. "Where have you looked, Eva?"

"I sent him out for firewood as soon as I noticed the storm clouds rolling in. He's had more than enough time to be back. I called for him and then looked for him in the barn. That's when I found the envelope. I'm so worried about him, Rachel. Where could he be?"

Rusty pushed open the screen door and looked out

into the rain. "Brannigan. I figure he went after Brannigan."

Chapter Twenty

Jack's heart kept pace with Ace's hoofbeats as he pounded his way up the trail to the ranch. Out of the corner of his eye, he watched the river rise as the torrential rain continued. He had known a man once who got caught in a flash flood, and he didn't relish the idea of that happening to him. He slowed Ace when they reached the steep embankment near Evangeline's property. The horse slipped and slid backward as he grappled his way up the muddy trail.

Jack couldn't explain it, but with every fiber of his being, he knew something was wrong at the ranch. When he saw that snake on the trail, he felt it must be a sign from God that his instincts were correct. Something had happened, or someone was in danger. He hadn't prayed since he was a boy but he knew God's word. In his youth, his mother read to him and his brother Jesse and made them memorize scripture. He knew God was with him and, now especially, he felt His presence.

The trail was washing out fast. Jack kicked Ace's sides hard, urging him to make it to the top of the embankment. Ace gave it his all, but lost his footing, sliding down to the bottom again. The sky was so dark that Jack had a hard time seeing where he was going. He knew he must find another path over the rise.

He reined Ace under a tree for a moment, looking for another likely path over the embankment. Lightning streaked the sky and Jack moved away from the tree, which would act as a lightning rod. No sooner had he moved back onto the trail, than another bolt forked down to earth. Before his eyes, a tree a hundred yards down the trail exploded as if ignited by sticks of dynamite, sending large branches flying and splitting the trunk in two. The massive smoldering trunk now lay across the trail.

He maneuvered Ace around the trunk and nearer to the ever-rising Little Blue River. Black Jack Brannigan was not a man given to panic, but he was running out of options. The trail was washing out, the embankment to his right was impassible, and the river to his left was rising fast.

Ace picked his way through the high brush when another flash of lightning lit the riverbank. At that moment, Jack thought he saw an animal scurrying near the water but dismissed it. As they drew nearer, he heard howling over the din of the storm.

Another streak of lightning illuminated the darkness ahead of him and Jack could make out a dog running back and forth across a washed-out section of the riverbank. He guided Ace closer until he could see the soaked and bedraggled Chester frantically barking at something beyond his sight.

"Chester! What in the world are you doing here in this storm, fella?" He dismounted and walked to the riverbank to see what had Chester so riled up. As he squatted in the semi-darkness, he saw a tiny hand gripping the exposed root of an old tree. In horror, he bent further down over the churning, rushing water and saw Noah's terrified face, as he held on for dear life, water rushing around his shoulders.

"Hold on, son. I'm gonna get you out of there!" Jack lay down on his chest and extended his hand but couldn't quite reach the boy. "Hold on, Noah!"

Jack hurried to Ace, took a rope from his saddle, and tied one end to the pommel, and the other end around his waist. He slid down the embankment and grabbed Noah's hand tight, pulling him into his arms.

"Back, Ace, back!" he shouted, unsure whether the horse would understand what he wanted him to do. As if on cue, Chester ran to Ace's hind leg and nipped it, causing him to whinny and back up. Soon Jack and Noah were on the river bank, shivering but safe.

Noah clung to Jack's neck with all his strength as Jack carried him to Ace's side. "You're okay, son." He untied the rope and pulled a poncho from his bedroll. He wrapped Noah in it and sat him in the saddle. Jack swung up behind the child, unbuttoned the slicker he wore, and secured it around the boy as well. "Let's go home."

Noah looked up at him with trusting eyes. Rain spattered his face, but he smiled.

Jack nudged Ace and they rode on through the mud and brush along the riverbank, Chester slogging along behind.

He estimated he had ridden nearly two miles past Evangeline's property before the ridge disappeared and he was able to get back onto level ground again. He turned and backtracked, heading again to Evangeline's ranch.

~

After more than two hours of searching, Evangeline met Rusty at the house. "It's no good, Rusty. We've got to get a search party." Evangeline stood before the kitchen stove, drenched and shaking. "We can't find him, and soon it will be pitch dark."

Rusty gripped the back of a chair and shook his head. "No, Miss Eva." He looked at her with real fear in his eyes. "You don't understand. We don't have time to ride into town and form a search party. Every minute counts right now."

Rachel handed him a steaming mug of coffee and then gave another mug to Evangeline. She sipped it and stared out the window.

Rusty drained his cup and set it back on the table. "Evangeline, that river is rising fast. It's already at flood stage, I'd imagine. We have to find him now, or we may not find him at all." He ran his hands over his face. "Rachel and me will get lanterns out of the shed and put oil in them. You get into dry clothes."

Evangeline couldn't remember ever hearing Rusty call her by her given name, but hearing him say it reminded her she was not alone – she had friends as close as family.

Near exhaustion and half-crazed with fear, she went into her bedroom and stripped off her wet dress and petticoat. Turning to her closet, Evangeline started to pick out another dress, when her eyes fell on the old shirt, pants, and boots she'd been wearing the day she met Jack Brannigan. She grabbed them and pulled the trousers on. After getting a jacket to wear under her slicker, she turned the doorknob and went back into the kitchen.

Heavy footsteps sounded on the back porch and Evangeline turned to face the door, expecting to see Rusty come in with the lanterns.

The door flew open and slammed against the wall. Jack stood in the doorway holding Noah in his arms. His black slicker whipped around him in the blast of chilly wind and rain.

"Jack! Noah!" She ran to them and threw her arms around Noah. "Are you okay? Jack, where did you find him? Rusty and I have been searching for hours."

"I'll tell you all about it, Evangeline, but let's get him into some dry clothes and in bed. He's been through one devil of a bad day."

Jack carried Noah into his bedroom and peeled the wet slicker from his drenched and muddy body. Evangeline grabbed the blanket from his bed and wrapped it snugly around his shoulders. She drew him into a tight hug. "Dear Lord, Noah. You have no idea how worried I've been about you. Thank God you're okay."

She stood and turned to Jack, the tears flowing freely now. "Thank you for bringing Noah home."

Jack shook his head gently. "You never have to thank me for this, Evangeline. I was every bit as worried about Noah as you were."

"And your money. Thank you with all my heart, but I can't keep it. The mere gesture means more to me than you'll ever know, but you take it with you." She touched his face, running her fingers down his stubbly cheek. "We'll be okay here."

"No, that money is for you and the children. You

may never recover what Wainwright stole from you. I want the money to be used to help build this ranch."

"What about your dream? Your gambling palace?"

He cupped her face. "My dream is right here. I know that now. Please let me stay and help you here, Evangeline. Let me help you raise these children. I love them." He gently kissed her face. "I love you."

Noah let out a whoop that caused Evangeline to jump three inches. "Yes, Miss Eva, we want Jack to stay! We want to stay with you and Jack forever."

Jack held her closer and spoke gently into her ear. "What about you? Do you love me enough to overlook all my flaws and forgive my past? I'm not perfect, and I never will be."

"I'm not looking for perfect. I'm looking for committed."

He kissed her tenderly on the forehead. "Listen to me, Evangeline. I've spent the last ten years on riverboats and in smoky saloons. Believe me when I tell you I've searched my heart and I know I want to be with you and the children. When I was riding away from you today, I was the most miserable man on the face of this earth. If you want me out of here now, you'll have to drive me out with a shotgun."

Tears filled her eyes as she slid her hands down his rain slicker, fingering the buttons. "That's what I've been waiting to hear, Jack. I want you, too. Please stay with us."

Noah jumped up and ran to them, wrapping his arms around them both. "Oh, what a happy day," he said. "The happiest day I've had in a long, long time."

Epilogue

Early September 1875

Mrs. Jack Brannigan stood on her front porch and breathed in the scent of freshly mown hay. Young colts played in the pasture with their mothers, others rested under the shade of a wide oak tree.

Evangeline watched as her husband and newly adopted children crossed the yard, hurrying toward the house. Carrie toddled beside Jack, holding onto his hand. Noah ran ahead and scrambled up the porch steps. Evangeline couldn't hold back her joyful laughter when she saw her family coming toward her. God had been so good to her, and she thanked Him every day for His blessings.

"Mother, Mother! Guess what?" Noah pointed to the barn, breathless. He nearly tripped up the steps.

Evangeline laughed again. "Calm down, Noah. What's the big news?"

Rachel opened the door and walked out onto the porch, the door snapping shut behind her.

"Jack says Scarlett is going to foal."

Evangeline raised her eyebrows and smiled the tiniest of smiles. "Scarlett is going to foal? Sounds like there'll be lots of new babies around this place before long."

Jack turned to Evangeline ever so slowly, a look of confusion on his face.

Rachel crossed her arms and giggled under her breath. "Yes, this ranch is growing by leaps and bounds."

A light came into Jack's eyes as a giant grin split his face. Before he could say a word, though, the sound of approaching hoofbeats caused everyone to look down the lane. Rachel shaded her eyes with a hand. "It looks like Mr. Benson from the telegraph office."

Mr. Benson jumped down from his horse and pulled an envelope from his pocket. "Telegram for Miss Rachel Rios."

Everyone looked at Rachel. "Miss Rios?" Jack asked in confusion.

Rachel stepped forward slowly. "Rios is my maiden name."

She took the envelope from the delivery man, her hand shaking. Did a telegram ever bring good news? She opened it, trembling.

Evangeline and Jack stood silently, waiting.

Rachel read the missive and looked up from the page, her face pale and worried. "It's from my sister, Teresa. My Papa is very ill and not expected to live. Rusty and I must go to Sonora immediately."

Evangeline rushed to her friend's side, concern knitting her brows together. "Go to your father right away. Jack and I will be fine. We can hire a few more hands while you're gone." She put an arm around Rachel's shoulder and squeezed her close.

Rachel threw a hand to her mouth. "I must go tell Rusty, immediately." She hurried down the steps and ran toward their cabin.

Jack came to Evangeline's side. "I hope her father will be okay." He smiled softly.

"I hope so, too, my darling. But I can't think about anything right now, except life. This ranch is full of life and growth and happiness. No matter what tomorrow brings, today I'm the happiest and most blessed woman on earth. I have everything I've ever dreamed of and more."

Jack picked up Carrie and pulled Noah near to their side. "This is our family. Jack and Eva, Noah and Carrie."

She smiled up at him. "And soon we'll be joined by little John Aaron or Rebecca."

Jack beamed. "A few months ago, I never would have imagined that this would be my life…that I could be this peaceful and content. Yes, God has blessed us beyond all measure."

THE END

13499655R00115